β

Ways to Entertain the Family When Stranded by a Blizzard

by Edmund Fairfax

- ✔ In the presence of your whole family, spontaneously ask your dinner guest stranded by the snowstorm—the one you've loved for years—to marry you. One exception: Know the Heimlich maneuver.

- ✔ Propose a marriage of convenience to your new bride and swiftly call the judge and a front-end loader.

- ✔ Enjoy a snowball fight with your new family.

- ✔ Don't forget to buy your new bride a wedding ring. The backwards nature of your courtship shouldn't throw you off.

- ✔ Kiss away your new wife's worried frown.

- ✔ Plan a dynamite wedding night!

Dear Reader,

During the eighteen years my husband and I and the kids lived in Austin, Texas, it snowed only twice—and melted the next day in both cases. So you can imagine our excitement our first winter in North Carolina, when we learned a major snowstorm was on the way. Unfortunately we couldn't have been less prepared. We had no rock salt nor sand for the sidewalks, no shovel to clear them and perilously few supplies.

Gamely, we ran out to get milk, bread and a bag of rock salt. (We didn't get a shovel because we didn't really think we'd need one.) We put our eldest daughter on a plane back to college. And settled in for a few inches.

The "few inches" turned into the Blizzard of '96 delivered in three separate back-to-back storms that closed schools and businesses for a week. During that time, as my family and I struggled to dig our way out of the driveway with a garden shovel, a hoe, a rake and other assorted garden tools, I found myself doing plenty of daydreaming.

What if a runaway bride, a schoolteacher on a fieldtrip and a young mother with her baby got stranded by a snowstorm, at the worst possible times, in the best possible places, with the men of their dreams? The result: Three new romantic comedies—SNOWBOUND BRIDE, HOT CHOCOLATE HONEYMOON and SNOW BABY.

I hope you enjoy reading all three books in my new trilogy "Brides, Babies & Blizzards" as much as I enjoyed writing them.

Best wishes, always,

Cathy Gillen Thacker

(who now has two shovels and a bag of rock salt, "just in case")

Cathy Gillen Thacker

SNOW BABY

Harlequin Books

TORONTO • NEW YORK • LONDON
AMSTERDAM • PARIS • SYDNEY • HAMBURG
STOCKHOLM • ATHENS • TOKYO • MILAN
MADRID • WARSAW • BUDAPEST • AUCKLAND

ISBN 0-373-16721-0

SNOW BABY

Chapter One

The sounds of Sesame Street songs filled the car as twenty-six-year-old Emily Bancroft glimpsed in the rearview mirror, where the single most important person in her life was snuggled in a powder blue snowsuit and matching cap and strapped safely into a padded leather safety seat. "How are you doing, sweetheart?" she asked affectionately.

In response, one-year-old Bobby Bancroft banged his rattle against the little armrest and babbled a stream of highly charming but completely unintelligible baby talk, complete with pauses, voice inflections and sophisticated intonations.

"That good, hm?" Emily asked cheerfully as she turned the windshield wipers up another notch against the blowing wind and increasingly fat, wet flakes of snow. "Well, it won't be long now. We're almost there."

"Bah!" Bobby shouted gleefully in response, dropping his rattle and waving both hands high above his head. "Bah!"

"Thirsty?" Emily asked with a grin. She wasn't surprised her blue-eyed, dark-haired angel was demanding his bottle. It had been almost two hours since their last stop. Eight hours total on the road. Ten hours since they'd seen their last glimpse of their Maryland home. And through it all her only son had been a real trouper.

Keeping one hand on the wheel and both eyes on the road, Emily reached in the diaper bag beside her. Her fingers curved around the bottle of apple-pear juice she'd packed. She worked off the cap and the insulated cozy, slipped her arm over the seat and handed it back. Bobby's tiny hands brushed hers as he cheerfully babbled some more—no doubt telling her how much he was looking forward to a long gulp of his favorite beverage.

"Do you have a good hold on it?" Emily asked. When she was sure he did, she let go. Seconds later, the chattering stopped and she heard him slurping away on his bottle.

Emily slowed her station wagon as she came upon yet another magnificent horse farm, surrounded by an immaculately kept white split rail fence. It was like something out of a storybook. "Do you see that, Bobby?" she asked, aware they were now deep in Kentucky horse country. "This is Somerset Farm. That means we're only a couple of miles away from the Fairfax Farm." And not a moment too soon, either, Emily thought with ever-escalating relief. The blizzard they'd thus far managed to elude was quickly descending upon them. There was an inch of snow on the ground now. And from the looks of the dense white clouds overhead there were buckets more to come.

"Hahsees—" Bobby said, dropping his bottle onto his lap, and pointing excitedly at the sleek and handsome horses with the shiny dark brown coats and heavy black manes. "Hahsees!"

"Yes, honey," Emily said, glancing at the fenced-in pasture her son had pointed out. "I see the horses. The grooms are taking them inside, aren't they?"

Bobby replied with another unintelligible string of excited words. Emily drove past a series of beautifully maintained horse barns, another fenced pasture and another and another, and then suddenly the white split rail fence of Somerset Farm turned abruptly to dark brown. There was a small elegantly crafted sign that said, Fairfax Farm, Sweet Briar, Kentucky, Established 1909, and after that a small, one-lane drive leading to a cottage that was set far back from the road.

As Emily turned down it, her snow tires slid an instant before once again snugly gripping the pavement beneath.

She tensed, aware the roads were getting bad.

Nevertheless, she couldn't leave this part of the country for good before she made amends to Edmund Fairfax and his eight-year-old daughter Chloe in person.

"Heaven knows I don't want to do this," Emily told Bobby with a beleaguered sigh as they closed in on the small, charming caretaker's cottage where Edmund Fairfax and his daughter Chloe had resided for the last week. "But circumstances have left us no choice."

"HI," EMILY BANCROFT said softly the moment Edmund Fairfax opened the door of the caretaker's cottage. She lifted a leather-gloved hand before he could voice his surprise at finding her on his doorstep. "Don't say it. I know I'm early—almost a week."

Edmund regarded the twenty-six-year-old widow of his boyhood friend. Though they had corresponded numerous times over the past year, after the sudden deaths of his wife and her husband, his job in Seattle hadn't allowed him to actually see Emily since her wedding to Brian two and a half years ago. To his surprise, the five-foot-six-inch beauty was lovelier than he had imagined she would be after all she'd been through, and at the same time, somehow more fragile, too. Yet the essential things about her—the thick silky waves of her shoulder-length raven hair, her high rosy cheeks, straight nose and luscious full mouth, the thick dark velvety lashes that framed her intelligent sea blue eyes—none of that had changed. True, her figure was a little more full since giving birth, her breasts larger, her hips slightly curvier, but the overall slenderness of her feminine frame was intact. Her skin was golden and glowing and, as in the past, she radiated breezy, natural beauty in a healthy girl-next-door way.

"Is everything okay?" Edmund asked as he ushered Emily and her baby boy in out of the cold.

"Actually, no." A little rush of breath escaped her soft, parted lips as Emily shifted Bobby to her other hip. Snowflakes dotted her shoulders, face and hair. "Which is why I've come." Emily paused. "I'm sorry, Edmund. I know it's awfully short notice. *Especially* since I'm the one who convinced you not to even advertise the position and give it to me instead. But I can't take the job as Chloe's nanny after all."

Edmund Fairfax felt his hopes to have his life return to some semblance of normalcy crumble. His daughter needed a mother figure around. A soft, gentle, giving woman to take Lindsey's place in her life. And he had thought—hoped—he'd found her in Emily.

"Are your in-laws giving you more trouble?"

"You guessed it." Emily grimaced.

Not that this was any surprise, Edmund thought, as he took in the clean, sexy fragrance of Emily's perfume. He and Emily had both known, going in, the upper-crust couple would not approve of their grandson's mother working as a nanny, no matter what the circumstances, or how well Emily and Bobby would be treated by him and Chloe as members of the family.

"So you've decided to return to teaching third grade instead?"

"No." Emily frowned. "At least not yet. I'm still thinking specifically about what I want to do. I just know I can't work here." Her expression softened apologetically. "I don't want to put you and Chloe in the middle of the ongoing unpleasantness between the Bancrofts and myself."

Edmund understood that. Inwardly, he commended her for her thoughtfulness. And yet… His brow furrowed. "Are you sure that's all it is?"

"Why?" Emily asked, abruptly looking a bit edgy. She took a seat on the overstuffed chintz sofa, settled Bobby on her knee and loosened the strings of his knit cap.

Because the evasiveness in your eyes tells me there's something else—some other complication— you're not telling me about, Edmund thought as he watched Emily unzip Bobby's snowsuit.

"Don't tell me you went to the main house first,"

he continued, only half joking. Had his mother done something to mess this up, too?

Emily shook her head as she finished removing a fidgety Bobby's outerwear. "I came straight to the cottage." When he continued to fuss, Emily let Bobby sit on the rug in front of her. "Why? What would've happened if I had gone to the main house?"

You'd have met my well-meaning but hopelessly meddling mother, Edmund thought, *and probably run as fast as you could the other way.* But not wanting to tell Emily that, when she was already inclined to bolt, he merely shrugged. "Nothing, I—"

Emily glanced briefly at Bobby, who was exploring the faded colors of the Aubusson rug with his fingertips, then turned her gaze back to Edmund. "Yes?" she prodded.

But before he could say anything, Chloe bounced into the room, her sable brown curls swirling around her face. She promptly sat down next to Bobby. "Daddy's worried 'bout what Grandma Maureen mighta said, 'cause Grandma Maureen doesn't want us to have a nanny."

"She doesn't," Emily parroted dryly.

"No," Chloe said seriously as she offered her hand for Bobby to clutch. "She wants us to live in the main house with her. But Daddy doesn't want to do that anymore, on account of Grandma Maureen's always trying to fix him up with some woman he doesn't want to be fixed up with."

Emily chuckled out loud at that bit of information and Edmund found himself flushing despite himself. "Chloe—" he reprimanded gently.

"Daddy, can I show little Bobby my stuffed animals?"

Welcoming the abrupt but timely change of subject, Edmund nodded his permission.

As Chloe ran to get them from the kitchen, she explained to Emily over her shoulder, "I brought them all out." She dashed back with her Pooh, Tigger and Eeyore gathered in her arms. "Daddy made tea for my tea party. But I don't get to drink real tea, only he does. I only get to drink apple juice." Chloe carefully set her stuffed animals down for Bobby to play with. "Can you and Bobby come to my party?" she asked eagerly.

"Oh, honey, we'd love to but—" Emily looked out the window. Her expression became worried. "The snow is starting to come down rather hard, isn't it?" She picked up Bobby's snowsuit and cap. "Which is exactly why Bobby and I should be on our way."

"No," Edmund corrected firmly but gently. "It's why you should stay here, at least for a night or two." She tensed at the suggestion and he continued amiably, "Haven't you been listening to the weather?"

Emily nodded. "An hour ago they said the brunt of the storm was going to hit one hundred and fifty miles east of here. Only a couple of inches was predicted for central Kentucky."

"They've since revised the forecast. We're now expected to get up to a foot of snow from the record blizzard that's moving its way up the East Coast. And since it's only been snowing here for an hour and we already have an inch on the ground, I'd venture they're right."

"Oh, dear." Emily placed cap and snowsuit back on the sofa.

Chloe tugged on Emily's sleeve. "Can Bobby have some of my apple juice?"

Emily smiled. "Actually, he already has a bottle of apple-pear juice in the car—but he can have that."

Chloe ran to get one of her storybooks and sat back down on the floor to play with Bobby. "Tell me where Bobby's bottle is and I'll go get it," Edmund said.

Emily was already tying the belt of her long, camel-colored wool coat. "That's okay. I'll do the honors," she said as she searched out her car keys and inched on her gloves. "If you could just keep an eye on Bobby for me for a moment—"

Edmund caught another whiff of her clean, sexy fragrance as she passed. "Sure."

"Mommy will be right back, honey."

Thoroughly happy where he was, Bobby did not protest her departure. Emily turned up her collar against the cold and slipped out.

Edmund sat down next to Bobby and Chloe. As he studied the raven-haired toddler, he thought how long it had been since he'd held a little one. *Too long.* His heart ached at the thought he would never have another child.

Chloe wrapped herself around Edmund's knee. "He's cute, isn't he, Daddy?" she asked on a wistful sigh.

"Very," Edmund admitted as he watched Bobby babble something eloquent—and completely unintelligible—to Chloe's Pooh bear. His face scrunched up in fierce concentration, Bobby reached for a red plastic block. Finding it out of his reach, he used Edmund's leg for leverage and pushed himself up to a standing position. Grinning triumphantly, he bobbed up and down, as if trying to propel himself into motion.

"Look, Daddy," Chloe said, fascinated. "Bobby's gonna walk!"

Bobby continued to bounce and look in the direction he wanted to go. Edmund held out a hand to assist. Bobby dropped backward, landing on his diaper-clad bottom with a thunk.

"Guess he's not gonna walk," Chloe said, disappointed, as Bobby rolled onto his tummy and crawled to what he wanted. He smiled and gurgled as he brought the red block to his mouth for further exploration.

"Maybe next time," Edmund said.

"I wish they could stay with us."

"I do, too," Edmund admitted. *You don't know how much.* He'd been incredibly lonely since Lindsey had died. Having Emily and Bobby there—knowing they were in the same boat—would have been nice. He and Emily could have shared what it was like to lose a spouse you loved more than life, and become a single parent overnight. The kids could've bonded, too.

"So how come Ms. Bancroft doesn't like us?" Chloe asked Edmund with heart-wrenching honesty, clearly feeling shunted around and abandoned all over again.

Emily came back inside, appearing windblown and slightly out of breath. A bulging diaper bag and a cloth sack of baby toys were slung over her shoulder. She'd obviously caught Chloe's remark; regret was etched on the pretty features of her face. "You can call me Emily, sweetheart. And I do like you, Chloe, very much," Emily told her gently as she set her things down.

"Then why don't you want to stay and be my

nanny and help me with my lessons from my school in Seattle? Especially,'' Chloe continued, looking both confused and hurt, ''when Daddy said you were as excited about coming here as we were about having you here?''

Emily shot Edmund a hesitant look that let him know in an instant she wasn't any happier about opting out of their arrangement than he was, before she returned her glance to Chloe's. ''It's…complicated,'' she said finally, as a flush highlighted her cheeks.

''Probably too complicated for your ears, young lady.''

Edmund confirmed in the tone of voice that let Chloe know that subject was closed for her. Wanting to talk to Emily himself, he looked at her for permission. ''Is it all right if we let Bobby stay on the floor with Chloe while we go over here?'' He indicated the table in the adjacent breakfast nook.

''Sure. Just let me give him some of his toys, too, and the rest of his bottle—'' While she made sure Bobby was settled, Edmund poured them both some tea. They took their seats at the cozy table by the window. He glanced at the kids, who were playing beautifully, then moved to take charge of the situation. ''What exactly has happened to change your mind? Is it the salary?'' It had to be something more than what she'd said thus far, since the disapproval of Brian's parents was something she'd been dealing with from the very beginning of her relationship with their son.

Emily shook her head. ''The salary you've offered is more than generous.''

''The location, and the fact we're so far from the city, then? Because if that's it, I'm planning to return to Seattle just as soon as I get things straightened out here with the family business—"

"Now that you're here and have had a chance to assess things, how long do you think that's going to take?" Emily asked, knowing originally Edmund had estimated anywhere from a week to a month or so.

Edmund frowned. "I'm not sure. It may be two months or more. Just depends on how quickly I can get things turned around." He paused. "Is the fact we're going to be here a lot longer than I originally thought troubling you?"

Emily stirred sugar into her tea. "No. I like living out in the country as well as the city."

"Then...?"

Steam from the tea caressed her face as Emily lifted the bone china cup to her lips and, still avoiding his eyes, took a delicate sip. "I'm just thinking farther south would be better."

Edmund studied the tense set of her femininely-shaped chin. "Do you have another job lined up?"

"Well, no." Emily squared her slender shoulders, as if girding up for battle. She turned her laser bright eyes back to him. "But I'm sure I'll have no difficulty finding one."

Edmund was sure she wouldn't, either. And that meant he only had one shot to make this work. He leaned forward urgently. "I really would like you to give it a try here," he said softly.

Emily tucked a lock of thick raven hair behind her ear. "I thought I explained this just isn't going to work out for Bobby and me."

He wasn't going to change her mind about the larger issues. Maybe he could persuade her on the smaller points. "Nevertheless, you and your son would be a lot safer here with us until the weather clears."

Emily hazarded another look outside the priscilla-curtained bay window, and saw—as did he—that the snow was coming down all the harder. "How far is it to Lexington from here?" she asked, her delicate brow furrowing.

"An hour, when the weather's good. The way it's snowing now you may as well quadruple the driving time assuming the roads between here and there don't shut down entirely."

Emily bit her lip. "What about hotels?"

"The closest is about thirty miles from here," Edmund replied as he poured them both more of the hot, fragrant tea. "It's located next to a truck stop on the interstate highway, and if you don't mind my saying, the crowd that frequents the place is kind of rough. It's no place for a lady or a baby."

Emily's head lifted. "Really, we don't want to impose."

"Then how about an even trade? I'll offer our gold star accommodations—" Edmund made a sweeping gesture that encompassed the cottage around them "—complete with meals, free. If you, in turn, will at least give the job a try for the length of time you're here."

Emily mulled over the suggestion. "You don't pull any punches, do you?" she murmured, not half as displeased as he had feared she might be.

It was time to lay all his cards on the table. Edmund leaned forward intently. "I know what I need here, Emily. I know what Chloe needs. And I think you and Bobby are it."

Emily fell silent, for a moment studying the man

who would've been her employer. She'd known she liked him from the first time they'd met, two and a half years ago at her wedding to Brian. The fact they'd both lost their spouses the previous winter in sudden, tragic accidents had added another bond. It had been Edmund's letters, written sporadically over the last few months, that had helped pull her out of her grief. His offer to hire her as nanny to his daughter, when Chloe's old nanny suddenly developed health problems and had to quit, had pulled Emily toward a new—and necessarily different—life.

But none of that, compelling as it was, had prepared her for seeing him in person again. None of that had prepared her for the sheer impact of the ruggedly handsome face, dark sable brown hair, and penetrating sable brown eyes of this sexy, well-to-do dad. None of that had prepared her for his physically fit six-foot frame or naturally athletic grace, nor the tender understanding and affability he displayed toward not only his child, but hers. Edmund Fairfax was a man who genuinely liked kids—and women—and people in general. He was a man who'd grieved every bit as deeply as he had loved. A man who was struggling to find his way to happiness again, just as she was. He was also smart, sophisticated, protective and gallant in an old-fashioned, Cary Grant way. He was everything she could ask for in a good male friend, and she found herself yearning to simply stay here with him. So why was she trying to run away from the shelter he offered when he'd made it clear he only wanted to help her, as some sort of last, gallant favor for Brian?

Was it because he made her feel so alive again? Or

was there something more here, something else she didn't want to see?

"The question is, Emily," Edmund said in a low, husky voice as he reached over and took both her hands in his warm, callused ones. "What do you want here? What do you need?"

In short, Emily thought, as she curled her fingers into his, *a safe place to stay. Plus, time to figure out what to do next.* Where better for either than right here? After all, realistically, what were the chances her in-laws or the process server from the family court in Maryland would find her if she did stay? Emily wondered.

She hadn't told her in-laws exactly where she was planning to take a job as a nanny. The discussion with the Bancrofts had never gotten that far. They had exploded at just the thought of her leaving the Maryland area and-or wanting to move on with her life. And heaven knew, this cozy cottage had to be a lot better for Bobby than a cold, sterile, maybe even dangerous hotel room.

"Emily?" Edmund prodded gently, still waiting for her answer.

The kindness in his face was enough to prod her to go with her instincts. "All right. I'll stay," Emily relented. "But only until the blizzard is over."

Edmund grinned, victorious, and sat back just as a knock sounded at the door and a handsome sixty-something woman in an elegant fur coat, pillbox hat and soft leather boots breezed in. She was followed by a similarly dressed, much younger woman with traffic-stopping movie starlet looks and dazzling silver-blond hair. "Edmund, darling, look who stopped by!" the first woman announced cheerfully.

"Hello, Mother." Edmund nodded at the first woman. Then—more stiffly still—the second. "Selena." Edmund reached behind him to lace an arm about Emily's waist and pull her forward. "I'd like you both to meet Emily Bancroft. Emily, this is my mother, Maureen Fairfax. And the niece of our neighbors, Selena Somerset."

"Hello." Emily nodded cordially at both in turn.

"Emily's gonna be my new nanny," Chloe piped up.

Maureen Fairfax shot her son a look. "I thought we had discussed this, Edmund."

"Actually, Mother, I think you discussed." Edmund angled a thumb at his chest and grinned wryly. "I don't think I got a word in edgewise."

"You obviously didn't listen, either." Maureen eased out of her fur and dropped it on the back of the sofa before turning to Emily and confiding, "No offense, dear, but Edmund does not need a nanny, he needs a wife, whether he realizes it or not!"

Edmund picked up his mother's fur and hung it safely out of Bobby's reach. "Mother—"

"I wouldn't worry about it. I'm not planning to be here all that long anyway," Emily interjected. She did not want to be put in the middle of a Bancroft family dispute, however inadvertently. She'd had enough of that with Brian's family.

"How long is not long?" Maureen asked cheerfully.

"Just a few days," Emily said, disappointed it wasn't going to work out after all. For a moment there—just a moment—as Edmund had held her hands in his she'd had a glimmer of hope it might.

"Unless, of course, Chloe and I can convince her

otherwise," Edmund replied firmly, taking center stage in the conversation once again. And, Emily noted, Edmund looked as though he were going to be working on that. A fact, Emily noted, that did not make Selena very happy.

Selena handed over the covered pie dish she'd brought in with her. "Well, I better be getting along home. I just wanted to drop this off for you and Chloe."

"Nice to see you, Selena. And thanks for the—" Edmund lifted the lid to check the fragrant, perfectly baked contents "—pie," he said politely.

Selena flushed with pleasure. "Your mother told me it was your favorite."

Edmund glared at his mother in exasperation.

Maureen smiled right back at him. "Edmund, maybe you could walk Selena to her car," she suggested firmly.

"Be happy to." Edmund ushered Selena.

Maureen turned to Emily. "Selena is the niece of our neighbor and my dearest friend. She loves horses and she adores Kentucky. She wants to settle in this area permanently and get married and have children." Maureen placed her hand over her heart and sighed dramatically. "In short, she is exactly what my son needs—if only he'll be open to the idea of a life with her."

Emily paused. "And you're telling me this because...?"

"I know my son. He never wants what he can easily have or should have for that matter."

A ripple of unease coursed down Emily's spine. No one would get close to Edmund and live happily ever after without this woman's approval. "I still don't understand how I figure into this," Emily reiterated cautiously.

"I saw how he looked at you just now and I know what that son of mine is thinking. If he starts a romance with you, it'll be enough to keep Selena away. But it's not true. Selena knows, every bit as well as I, that she and Edmund are fated to be together. And she's determined to stay next door with her relatives until he realizes it, too."

Shouldn't someone have asked Edmund what he wanted? Emily wondered.

Before they could continue their discussion, the back door to the cottage swung open. A vivacious-looking young woman with short sable brown hair and more than a passing resemblance to Edmund strode in. "Where's that brother of mine?"

"Out front," Edmund's mother replied. "Why? What's going on?"

"I've got to talk to him, that's what." Seeing Emily, the young woman in a long wool coat and a classic blue business suit extended a leather-gloved hand. "Hi. Gail Fairfax. And you're—"

"Emily Bancroft," Emily said with a smile.

"Edmund's new temporary nanny," Maureen added helpfully.

"Permanent, Mother," Edmund corrected coming back in.

Since when? Emily wondered. She'd only agreed to stay through the storm.

Maureen turned around to face her son, who was standing behind her. She did not look at all happy to see Edmund back so soon. "That was fast," Maureen observed with a lift of her patrician brow.

"I didn't want to delay Selena on account of the

snow." Edmund looked at his sister, as if surprised to see her there that time of day. "Everything okay?" he asked Gail with a solicitous frown.

His younger sister shook her head. "No, it's not. In fact, it's worse than ever!"

Now why does that not surprise me? Edmund thought.

Checking to make sure Chloe and Bobby were still playing happily with their toys, he guided his sister, mother and Emily to the breakfast nook table. "Sit down and tell me what happened."

Gail took a deep breath. "The Thurstons called my law office about half an hour ago. They've decided not to renew their contract to breed their mares here. They're going with Castlebrook Farm instead."

Edmund felt the blow like a punch to his gut. They were talking about a one hundred thousand dollar loss in farm revenue, and this was just the last in a string of similar disappointments since his father had died the previous spring. "But they've done business with us for the last twenty years!" he said.

Gail looked uncomfortable. "I know."

"Did they give any explanation why they're switching?" Edmund demanded.

Gail sighed. "You're not going to like it."

"Tell me anyway," Edmund insisted.

"The Thurstons said if you're not staying to run the farm permanently, they're going to take their business elsewhere permanently."

Edmund didn't know why it had suddenly all come down to him. His mother had worked side by side with his father, running the family's renowned horse-breeding business, the last forty years. True, their farm manager had recently quit in a dispute with her, but they still had a staff of over twenty-five employees to carry out the day-to-day operations. "Did you tell them I'm looking for a new farm manager now?" he asked Gail.

Gail nodded. "They don't care."

Edmund sat back in his chair, aware the weight of the family's reputation had never felt heavier to him than it did at that moment. "Have the Thurstons signed a contract with Castlebrook Farm?"

"No. Not yet. They were supposed to do so today, but with the weather being what it is, they couldn't get over there to go over the papers with the Castlebrook Farm's office."

Aware of Emily's eyes upon him, Edmund rose. "I'll call them."

"It's not going to do any good," Gail predicted with a sigh.

Edmund turned to face his younger sister grimly. "It has to. We can't afford to lose their business."

"WELL?" Gail and Maureen said in unison the moment Edmund got off the phone.

Edmund cast a glance at Emily, who had excused herself from the table to supervise the children at play. "The best I could do was get them to delay the decision until after they've met with me, retoured the facilities here and been to dinner."

His mother whipped an ink pen and a small leather-bound date book from her purse. "When will that be?" she asked efficiently. Edmund knew what she was thinking—a dinner party was something she could handle.

"Day after tomorrow, providing the roads are clear enough to make the drive."

His mother scribbled down a reminder. "I'll talk to Mrs. Hamilton about the menu," Maureen said.

Gail smiled. "And I'll have the legal papers ready to sign, just in case they decide to go with us after all."

Edmund nodded, relieved. He cast another look at Emily, who was seated on the couch, a child cuddled contentedly on either side of her. Both Chloe and Bobby were entranced with the lyrical, velvety sound of her voice, and the three of them looked so natural together—so content—he felt a lump grow in his throat. The longing to have a complete family again grew. His mother touched his arm lightly. "I'll expect you, Emily and the children to meet us up at the main house in one hour."

Emily shot a look at Edmund, then turned back to Maureen. "I think it'd be better, under the circumstances, since I'm going to be Chloe's nanny, if Bobby and I ate with the rest of the staff."

"Normally, I'd agree." Maureen smiled in kind. "Generally, the staff does not dine with the family here. But since you're going to be taking care of my only grandchild, I'd like to know you a little better."

Or in other words, Edmund thought grimly, Emily was up for an inquisition she obviously did not want.

Maureen and Gail said their goodbyes and left. Emily let Bobby climb back down on the floor to play with Chloe. Emily joined Edmund as he gathered up the tea things and carried them to the kitchen sink. "Your mother really disapproves of me staying here."

Only because it's interfering with her matchmaking plans. Edmund shrugged. "She'll get over it."

Emily tilted her chin. "Do you enjoy getting her goat?"

"I enjoy making my own decisions without her input." Edmund cast a glance out the window at the worsening weather. The snow was coming down fast and furious now. "We better get your things inside before any more snow piles up on your car."

Emily quickly headed for her coat. "I can do it."

Edmund had been reared to never let a lady carry anything when a man was there to do it for her. "No, I'll do it. You stay here and watch the children."

Evidently realizing this wasn't a battle she would win, Emily reluctantly relented.

While she watched, he brought in the high chair, playpen, two suitcases, one garment bag, two boxes of disposable diapers and a case of baby food. "The only thing left in the car is a leather satchel and a box of storybooks and toys. Do you need them?"

Emily nodded. "Yes." She bit her lip. "I do."

He went back, got them and carried them inside. The satchel and overflowing box in hand, he headed back toward the bedrooms at the rear of the cottage.

He inclined his head toward a small blue bedroom with a four-poster double bed that had been in his family for generations. "This is my room. And next to it, Chloe's." He indicated the room with the abundance of toys, white children's furniture, and pink gingham bedspread.

"Over here is where you and your baby will be staying." Edmund led the way into a sunny yellow bedroom with a single bed and bureau on one side, and a crib and changing table on the other. Edmund set down the overflowing box of toys and storybooks in the corner, where it'd be out of the way. "For now, at least, the two of you will have to bunk together."

"No problem." Emily smiled as Edmund plucked the satchel off the top of the box.

Edmund started to hand the satchel over to her, to put it where she wanted it. He frowned as the bulging case nearly fell open. "The clasp on this satchel seems to be working loose," he warned.

"That's okay. I'll take it," Emily said hurriedly, as he attempted to fix it.

Abruptly seeing where the tiny gold-plated screw on the bottom of the clasp had worked loose from its grooved anchor in the soft, worn leather, Edmund said, "I think I've got it—"

"Really, I—" Emily tried to take it from him before she'd given him a chance to make the repair. Afraid the fastening mechanism would fly apart and they'd lose the tiny parts somewhere in the rug, Edmund kept his hold on the satchel. She tugged anyway. The increased pressure on the satchel was all it took to separate the latch into pieces. The satchel suddenly flew open. A sheaf of papers, a laptop computer, and four thick bundles of crisp green currency spilled over the bed.

Chapter Two

The silence in the room was deafening. "I can explain," Emily said finally, as a hot flush of embarrassment crept into her cheeks. Darn it all, she didn't like feeling guilty when she'd done nothing wrong!

"Obviously," Edmund quipped wryly as he thumbed through the crisp new stacks of bills then tossed them haphazardly back on the bed. "Unless you just robbed a bank."

"Very funny." Emily rummaged around in her purse. She handed him a withdrawal slip from her bank in Maryland. "As you can see, I withdrew the money from my account early today."

"And you closed the account," he noted.

His hand brushed hers as he handed the bank paper back to her. At the touch of his skin on hers, a tingle of unaccustomed warmth swept through her.

"Why?" His sable brown eyes lasered in on hers, pinning her to the spot. "If you weren't planning to take the job here after all?"

Emily shrugged and tried not to think about how much she liked the crisp wintry fragrance of his aftershave. "I decided I'd like to move south," she told him honestly. "Maybe somewhere warm and tropical, where Bobby could play outside all year round."

That much Edmund could readily understand, Emily noted with relief, particularly with the current blizzardlike weather outside. The rest of her behavior he obviously found harder to accept, starting with her early, unannounced arrival at his cottage. His gaze roved her upturned face in a slow, leisurely manner she found all the more unnerving. "Why did you get cash, instead of a cashier's check?"

Good question, Emily thought, as she shifted her weight from foot to foot, *and one I'm not really certain I'm at liberty to answer.*

"You don't have to tell me," he said gently, capturing one of her hands in both of his, as another tense, awkward silence stretched between them.

Isn't that the truth? Emily thought.

"I think I know the answer to that, anyway," Edmund continued as he sat down on the bed and tugged her down to sit beside him. Behaving as if she were cooperating fully with his attempts to aid her, he continued to hold her hand. "You don't want to be traced, and a cashier's check could be traced. The question is," he continued, rubbing his thumb across the back of her hand, "why don't you want to be traced? You're a widow with a baby boy. Who could be looking for you or threatening you enough to the point you'd have to run? Especially today of all days."

Who indeed.

Edmund shrugged, released her hand and stood. Gallant to the core, he looked as if he'd stop at nothing to help her, whether she and Bobby asked for his assistance or not. "Well, there's an easy enough way to find out, I suppose," Edmund drawled as he headed for the phone on the nightstand.

"No, don't," Emily said urgently, as she leapt to her feet and caught his wrist. Edmund went very still as her fingers slipped down to curl imploringly with his. "I'll tell you," Emily said, dropping her tenuous hold on him and lifting both hands in a gesture of surrender. "Just please—" she whispered, her eyes misting with hot, desperate tears "—I beg of you— don't let anyone from my old life in Maryland know I'm here."

"I promise I won't," Edmund said as he gripped her shoulders and stared down into her face, "but in return you've got to level with me, Emily."

What he was requesting was only fair, Emily knew. She drew a deep, bolstering breath as she tilted her head back and looked up into his face. "Brian's parents want custody of Bobby. I've known it all along, I guess. They've tried repeatedly to get me and Bobby to move in with them."

"But you didn't want that." Emily slipped from his light, restraining hold and began to pace.

"No," Emily replied, shoving both her hands through her hair. "We don't get along all that well, under the best of circumstances, and that was the case even when Brian was alive."

"Don't feel bad." Edmund picked up the bundles of money, tossed them back into the satchel, and latched it for safekeeping. "He didn't get along all that well with them, either, as I recall."

Emily nodded, remembering. "We just have such different values," she murmured, as she stepped to the window and studied the steadily falling snow outside. She touched a hand to the window frame, and felt the ice-cold chill of the frame penetrate all the way to her soul. "But I could have dealt with that."

"Until...?" Edmund prodded, sensing there was more.

Emily swallowed again, hard. Though not entirely unexpected, this was such a humiliation; she hated discussing it, even with him. "I was tipped off late last night by a mutual friend that Whit and Andrea Bancroft are trying to have me declared an unfit mother, because I want to go back to work and build a new life for myself and Bobby, instead of move in with them. They planned to file papers with the court today, asking for immediate emergency custody of Bobby, while we all wait for a court date when the specifics of the case can be heard."

"You don't think a judge would have taken their complaint against you seriously!" Edmund exclaimed in a low, stunned voice.

Emily's heart pounded as she watched him saunter closer. If only that were true. But it wasn't, and she'd do well to remember that, as would Edmund. Taking a deep breath, she met his eyes and recited the facts of the situation, forcing him to face reality, as she had. "Money and influence shouldn't outweigh a mother's love for her child, but you and I both know that isn't always the case," she said sadly as he settled opposite her, resting one broad shoulder against the door frame. "The Bancrofts both inherited a ton of money from their families, whereas I'm living on the proceeds of Brian's life insurance, provided by the public school where he taught. Right now it's a matter of the haves and have-nots. I'm afraid the judge will look at what Whit and Andrea can give Bobby in terms of private schools and twice-yearly trips to Europe and the very best of everything, and determine he'll be better off with them than me."

Edmund frowned, knowing as well as she that money alone, and the things it bought, did not buy happiness. "If I remember correctly, Brian had some sort of trust in his name, worth a million or more."

"Yes, he did," Emily admitted stoically, "from his grandfather, but he hadn't come in to it yet, and right now, it's still tied up in probate."

"Who's the beneficiary?"

"Bobby—and-or his executor in Brian's estate—which at the moment is me."

"Then that trust should be considered in the deliberation by the judge," Edmund returned matter-of-factly.

"But what if it isn't?" Emily cried softly, feeling even more frazzled and bereft as she forced herself to go on. "What if the probate judge decides the trust should go back to Whit and Andrea and that *they* should administer the trust funds to Bobby, as they see fit? Then I'll still have very little to offer my son, in monetary terms, and they'll have the world." And then what?

Edmund frowned grimly in disapproval. "I don't understand. Why would Whit and Andrea *do this?*"

Emily shook her head—she'd asked herself the same thing many times, to no avail. "I think there are several reasons, but the most pressing is that they miss Brian and mourn his death terribly." As had she, for nearly a year. Only now she was ready to move on and they weren't. "Whit and Andrea see Bobby as their last remaining link to Brian. They want to raise Bobby as a Bancroft, without any influence from me, and they'll do anything they have to to ensure that happens. Including," she amended grimly, "lie about me."

"You could fight it. You're his mother, for God's sake!"

Emily released a wavering laugh. As if she had wanted to take off the way she had, leaving nearly everything she owned, including the equity in her small modest home, behind! "The Bancrofts have more money and connections than I could ever dream of having. There isn't a judge in all of Maryland who'd side with me against them," she said wearily, beginning to pace again.

Edmund paused to listen for the children, who— from the sound of it—were still playing happily together. He moved closer, keeping his voice low and urgent. "I can't believe that, if you've done nothing wrong."

"Well, join the club," Emily said, angling a thumb at her heart. "I didn't believe it either until I found out they were willing to drag me into court—say my judgment where my son was concerned was flawed to the point of being dangerous, for heaven's sake!—and declare me unfit to rear him, so a family court judge would grant them sole temporary custody of Bobby!" She rubbed her arms against the chill that had come up out of nowhere. "They knew I was planning to leave town early next week, and they knew they wouldn't have the same kind of clout if I were a resident in another state. So they pulled every string they could and made arrangements to have the case heard before I could take a job elsewhere."

"Sort of a preemptive strike," Edmund mused.

"Yes, to keep me from taking Bobby where I might get a fair hearing."

"So you left town. And cleaned out your bank account on the way."

Emily nodded. "I figured I'd be a lot harder to trace if I didn't use credit cards or checks."

"Do they know you planned to take a job here with me?"

"No." Emily heaved a sigh of relief. "Thank God we never got that far in our discussion. The moment I mentioned taking a job, where I could gain a little independence, earn a good salary and stay at home and be a mother to Bobby, they hit the roof." She shook her head and related miserably, "Heaven knows they never liked the fact that I was a schoolteacher or that I came from very modest circumstances, but they were livid at the thought of my taking a position as a nanny, and they absolutely forbid me to do so."

"The idea of you working as a domestic was embarrassing to them."

"Very," Emily affirmed tightly. "Which is silly, because taking good, loving care of a child is the most important job in the world. And having the luxury of being able to give lots of extra special care and loving one-on-one attention to children—like your Chloe and my Bobby—who've both already experienced such wrenching loss, well, it's really wonderful," she said softly, in a low tender voice that came straight from the heart. "In fact, I thought it might be really good for Bobby to grow up around another child who had also lost a parent at an early age. I thought it might help both him and Chloe feel less alone. And help them bond."

Emily could tell from the look on his face that Edmund had been hoping the same thing. It was one of the reasons he'd been so willing to hire Emily for the position of Chloe's nanny, despite the fact he—like her in-laws—had not initially been sure the wife of an old friend should take such a position. But she'd won him over when they'd talked more and he'd discovered their child-rearing philosophies meshed perfectly, as did their fierce protectiveness and abiding love for their children. He also knew, from the letters they had exchanged, after the deaths of their respective spouses, that she felt his loss, and Chloe's pain, the way few others did—because she'd experienced it, too.

"But Whit and Andrea don't see it that way," Edmund guessed, as he wreathed a comforting arm around her shoulder.

"No, they don't." Emily was quiet a moment, savoring the warmth and compassion in his touch, before she continued unburdening herself to him. "They have no problem with the fact I want to build a new, fulfilling life for myself, and in fact have encouraged me to do so, promptly—as long as I leave the rearing of Bobby solely to them. The fact I refused to abandon my child and sign him over to them has irritated them no end. And they weren't willing to work out any kind of compromise or middle ground that would allow us to coexist peacefully."

"That's a shame."

"Yes, it is," Emily said softly, reassured by the depth of understanding she saw in his eyes. Her voice trembled with the fire of her conviction. "Bobby should be able to love both his mother and his grandparents, without being caught in the friction between us, but that's exactly what has happened." She sighed, wondering—not for the first time—how she was ever going to get through this alone. "And the differences between us are so vast, I know it's only going to get worse as Bobby gets older." Her whole body tensed and she surged restlessly away from Edmund once again. "This custody battle is just the tip of the iceberg," she imparted beleagueredly as she raked her hands through her hair. "Brian's parents are so smothering and possessive they won't be satisfied until they've cut me completely out of my son's life.

"Unfortunately, because I made no secret of my plans to other friends, I know they will eventually be able to trace me to you." Emily swallowed, and for the first time since she'd entered the cottage, felt a tinge of regret—the last thing she'd ever wanted to do was drag him and his family into this. "That's the real reason I can't stay." *Even if I want to with all my heart.* "So like it or not, Edmund, as soon as this blizzard is over, and the roads are clear," she declared with a sad, weary sigh. "Bobby and I will have to be moving on, as planned."

"I LIKE HER, Daddy," Chloe enthused the moment they were alone. Dressed in her favorite green velvet dress and matching tights, Chloe dropped her shoes on the floor and climbed onto the center of his bed. Like him, she was nearly ready for dinner with Maureen and Gail at the main house; Emily and Bobby were in her room, dressing for dinner, too.

Hopping on to the center of the spread, Chloe began to bounce gently up and down, as if she were warming up for acrobatics on the trampoline. "And I like Bobby, too, Daddy. What about you?"

"I like them both," Edmund replied in a low, distracted voice as he mulled over which tie to wear with his dove gray dress shirt and charcoal suit—the funky navy, gray and white tie, peppered with horizontal rows of baseball players taking a swing or the discreet gray silk one he'd bought with the suit.

Chloe swiveled around to the left, still bouncing lightly, and jumped for a while facing that way. "A whole lot or a little?" Chloe asked.

"A whole lot," Edmund replied.

And although he'd been prepared for that, and had been prepared, in fact, to have a casual friendship with Emily based on their mutual forays into single parenthood, he had *not* expected to have an immediate physical and emotional reaction to her.

But he had.

And at the moment he wasn't quite sure what to do about it.

If she'd been going to take the position as Chloe's permanent nanny, he would've had no choice but to keep his hands off.

But she wasn't.

And that left the situation wide open.

How did you behave when you realized you were physically attracted to the wife of an old friend? Edmund wondered as he selected the gray silk tie and looped it around his neck. Never mind a woman just out of mourning...

"Emily's really, really nice," Chloe continued, as she stopped bouncing and sat down abruptly to put on her black patent leather shoes.

Yes, Edmund thought with a fierce protectiveness that stunned him, Emily was nice. Which in turn made what Whit and Andrea Bancroft were doing to her all the more inexcusable.

"And pretty, too," Chloe sighed contentedly.

No argument there, Edmund thought, as he lifted his shirt collar, slid the tie underneath, and then covered it up again. His pulse raced just thinking about her.

Chloe buckled her shoes, dashed over to where he stood in front of the mirror and did a quick pirouette. "Do you see how she fixed my hair for me?"

Edmund admired his daughter's precisely plaited sable brown hair. Unlike when he did it, the braid was perfectly straight and centered neatly on the back of her head. "That's a very nice braid," he said admiringly.

"A French braid," Chloe corrected. "Not an old regular one. And lookit—" Chloe pointed to her waist proudly "—how she tied the bow on my dress."

"It's perfect," Edmund agreed. Certainly a lot better than he could do. When it came to bows and braids, he was all thumbs. And likely to stay that way.

"I'm so glad she's going to be my nanny." Chloe released a satisfied sigh as she stood, watching, as Edmund tugged on his jacket.

If only that were the case, Edmund thought with a pang, acknowledging his own disappointment that Emily was planning to move on, son in tow, ASAP.

"And you know what else?" Chloe threw her arms about him and hugged him fiercely. "I love you, Daddy, so much."

Edmund's heart filled as he hugged her back. "I know you do, pumpkin," he said emotionally.

"But I've missed having a mommy," Chloe said, clinging all the harder.

"I know you have," Edmund said, gently touching

her cheek. *I've missed having a mother for you and a wife for me, too.*

Chloe loosened her bear hug on him and beamed up at him. "Having Emily here with us is gonna be like having a mommy and a baby brother, too."

Tell her it's not going to happen, after all. Tell her now. Try as he might, no words came, and Edmund remained silent beside her. His little girl was only eight, and already she'd had so much loss in her life. The past year had been hell for them both, with many more downs than ups. He'd despaired of ever filling her mother's place in her life. Or his own. And now that Chloe had finally found someone she responded to again, someone who did more than just take care of her needs, the way her previous nanny had, someone who made her smile, how was he going to tell her that it wasn't going to happen after all?

EMILY HAD JUST finished putting on her pearl earrings when the knock sounded on her bedroom door.

"Hurry up, Emily. We're waiting!" Chloe called impatiently from the hall.

Emily grinned as she heard Edmund shush his daughter.

"Take your time," he amended, more graciously, as she took a last final look in the mirror.

Knowing it was always better to be overdressed than under, she'd selected an elegant ecru brocade satin suit, with matching stockings and soft leather pumps. Her makeup was elegant and understated, her necklace a single strand of pearls. She'd brushed the thick unruly waves of her raven hair away from her face, caught it sleekly at her crown, then let it fall loose and free to her shoulders.

"Dinner won't be served for another hour," Edmund continued.

"That's okay." Deciding she looked more than okay—even for a hostess as demanding of her guests as Maureen Fairfax—Emily gathered up Bobby and, her heart pounding, glided forward to open the door. "We're ready," she announced as she cuddled Bobby closer and stepped out into the hall, where Edmund and his daughter waited.

Even as she smiled at the stunned look on his face, she couldn't help but note how incredibly good he looked, too.

"What?" she prodded teasingly, as his lips curved and his eyes darkened to a rich chocolate brown. "Did I forget something?" She could swear his gaze hadn't missed an inch of her.

"No." Edmund sighed admiringly, still taking her in from head to toe. "You look...spectacular."

"Thanks." Emily shifted Bobby, who was already reaching for Edmund, to her other side. Together, they walked out to the living room. Edmund grabbed their coats. "Maybe I should hold Bobby while you and Chloe slip on your jackets," he said.

Emily grinned. "Good idea."

Bobby babbled happily as Edmund took him in his arms.

"I think he likes you, Daddy," Chloe said, as Bobby patted Edmund's chin and spoke even more animatedly.

"I think so, too."

"That's good." Chloe beamed proudly. "'Cause I think he's as cute as can be, too."

Emily bundled Bobby in his snowsuit and cap. Thankfully his usual protest during this process was

minimal. Ducking their heads against the icy chill of
the blowing wind and snow, they all trooped cautiously out to the Jeep Edmund had warming in the
drive. "Normally, I'd walk up to the main house,"
Edmund explained, "but in this weather, with the
kids—"

"I understand and agree perfectly." Emily climbed
into the back with Bobby. Chloe climbed in front with
her dad. When everyone was buckled in, Edmund
drove past the horse barns and fenced pastures, all of
which were covered with a blanket of snow. Half a
mile or so later they reached the main house.

The sprawling white brick colonial was like something out of *Gone with the Wind.* Four huge pillars
lined the front of the elaborately landscaped two-story
mansion. The shutters and doors were painted a bright
cranberry red. Inside, the home glowed with welcoming light while outside snow drifted onto the porch
and piled upon the eaves.

"There's Grandma Maureen now!" Chloe said excitedly as the front door swung open. "And look!
Selena's here, too!"

"I thought you were headed home," Edmund com-
mented politely as the four of them rushed inside the
grand front hall.

Selena looked at Edmund like a cat savoring a bowl
of cream. She, too, had dressed to the nines, in a slim
low-cut black sheath that clung like a second skin to
her curvaceous body.

"Visibility was too poor to get to Somerset Farm
safely, so I turned back," Selena explained.

"And I asked her to stay for the duration of the
blizzard," Maureen added. "I decided we could use
the company."

We? Or Edmund? Emily pondered.

"Luckily, Selena still had her suitcases in her car," Maureen continued, "so even if we get socked in for days, Selena will have everything she needs, won't you dear?"

Selena nodded.

Chloe slipped out of her coat and tugged on her grandmother's sleeve. "Grandma Maureen," she whispered surreptitiously. "I'm hungry."

"I know you are, darling." Maureen bent and hugged Chloe warmly. "And dinner's all ready."

Maureen took the lead, ushering the group through the marble-floored hall and past a sweeping circular staircase, into the formal dining room. A high chair had been set up next to Emily's chair at a polished mahogany table. "This high chair used to be mine," Chloe bragged, as she sat down next to her daddy, on the other side of the table.

Emily smiled as she settled a sailor-suited Bobby into his seat. "Thank you for letting Bobby use it, Chloe."

Chloe grinned as Selena seated herself on the other side of Edmund. "You're welcome," Chloe replied cheerfully, while Gail and Maureen seated themselves, too.

Thankfully, during dinner, Edmund was able to cut Maureen's matchmaking short as he steered the conversation to the most mundane details of farm business. His sister Gail, an attorney who handled all the farm business and worked part-time as a justice of the peace, was only too happy to help him in his quest. By the time they'd all finished the delicious main course of roast chicken and wild rice, Chloe and

Bobby were both restless. And Selena, long but politely ignored, was clearly piqued.

"Perhaps the children would prefer their dessert upstairs in the playroom, while I supervise," Mrs. Hamilton, Maureen's housekeeper, said.

"That's an excellent idea," Maureen Fairfax said, then looked at Emily, as if for permission. Emily—having no idea about the facilities of the playroom, looked at Edmund.

He seemed to think it was okay. "I'll go up and see they're settled," he said.

No sooner had he, Mrs. Hamilton and the children left, then Maureen turned back to Emily. "You've been awfully quiet, dear."

Emily smiled as the plates were cleared. "I don't know an awful lot about breeding Thoroughbred horses."

"Really?" Selena said as generous slices of black forest cake were served. "That's a shame. I, on the other hand, love them, and would like nothing better than to make them my life's work."

"Then perhaps you should buy a Thoroughbred breeding operation of your own," Edmund advised, joining them again.

"Or marry into one," Maureen added coyly.

"That would be wonderful," Selena said, sending an adoring look Edmund's way.

"I'll see if I can drum up any eligible farm owners to introduce to you," Edmund murmured in a low, urgent voice.

Maureen laughed gaily. "I don't think that's what Selena had in mind, dear."

"I think he knows that, Mother," Gail interjected dryly, rolling her eyes.

"Perhaps we should change the subject," Edmund said tactfully.

"Good idea," Maureen decreed as everyone dug into their cake. "About the sleeping arrangements for Emily and her baby—"

Edmund sipped coffee, unperturbed. "I've already settled them in at the cottage."

Maureen pursed her lips and set down her own bone china cup in exasperation. "Darling, no—"

"Mother, yes," Edmund replied sardonically.

"To have you both under the same roof, single and unchaperoned in such a small cottage! Darling, people will talk!"

Edmund shrugged, no longer bothering to hide his annoyance, now the children were out of the room. "Then let them," he muttered cantankerously beneath his breath.

Maureen continued affably, "I insist Emily and Bobby sleep up here with us, at the main house."

"Mother, there's not much point in having a live-in nanny if the nanny is not under the same roof."

Even for a couple of days, Emily thought, aware she didn't want to bunk anywhere but with Edmund, either.

"There is still the matter of Emily's reputation to consider," Selena put in helpfully.

Yes, Emily thought irascibly, there was. She normally didn't care what people said about her, but with a custody case looming and the possibility existing the Bancrofts and their lawyers would soon catch up with her, she couldn't afford to be as cavalier as Edmund about what people thought or said, either here, or in Maryland, or anywhere else for that matter!

"I know," Edmund agreed, as he turned to give

Emily a warm, surprisingly adoring yet equally matter-of-fact look. "I've thought of that," he said, his sensual lips curving into a sexy smile. "And I think I've come up with a solution," he announced to one and all.

"And that is?" his mother prodded immediately, looking both curious and miffed, as was her compatriot, Selena.

Edmund looked at Emily. His dark brown eyes sparkled with mischievous lights as he stood and held out his hand to her. "I think—for a variety of reasons—that the two of us should just get married."

Chapter Three

Emily's mouth dropped open while pandemonium broke out all around them.

"You can't be serious!" Maureen gaped at her son.

Selena glared at the man she'd made no bones about wanting to marry herself. "This isn't funny, Edmund," she said stiffly.

"Oh, I don't know," Gail chuckled with sisterly glee as she perused her older brother with equal parts exasperation and admiration. "I, for one, am amused to see my normally serious brother act so recklessly."

Edmund looked at Emily. "Perhaps we should discuss this in private?" he said softly, no doubt reading the pique in her eyes.

At that moment, Emily had no desire to be alone with him, but the truth was, she wanted nothing better than to give him a piece of her mind. "Good idea," she said smoothly, circling the table to his side.

"If the kids need us, we'll be in the study," Edmund told one and all. "Otherwise," he paused significantly, "we'd appreciate a moment alone."

"Go, bro," Gail murmured, as Edmund escorted Emily out of the dining room, down a long parquet-floored hall, and into a huge room on the east side of the mansion. Stepping inside the double doors was like stepping inside a sanctuary. And it was clearly a man's abode. Floor-to-ceiling bookshelves lined the walls. The sumptuous saddle brown leather furniture was oversized, deep and inviting. In the center of the room was a massive walnut desk that was polished to a high sheen and looked as if it had been in the family for generations. An expensive leather swivel chair was behind it, and it was definitely a power seat, if there ever was one.

As Edmund shut the doors behind them, Emily's glance fell to the photos of magnificent Fairfax Farm bred horses, and then to an oil portrait hung over the white brick fireplace. She stepped beneath it for a closer look. The gold plate beneath it said Clayton Fairfax. "Is that your father?"

Edmund joined her on the hearth. "Yes."

He was a very handsome man. Rugged, imposing, and yet there was a gentleness in his eyes, not unlike his only son's, that she found very appealing. "You look a lot like him." They had the same sable brown hair and eyes, the same athlete's body, and sensually chiseled lips.

"Thanks," Edmund said, easily enough. "This was his office, when he was alive. He greeted visitors and did all the farm business right behind that desk. I thought Mother might redecorate when she took over the business after his death last spring, but she hasn't changed a thing."

Too aware of her host and would-be-employer for comfort, Emily glided away. "That's probably because she was waiting for you to come home and take his place," she said as she folded her arms in front of her and tucked them against her waist.

"That's not going to happen on any permanent basis," Edmund said firmly. "I'm only back to figure out what the problems are and help turn things around for her, then I'm out of here."

Emily arched a dissenting brow. "Your mother obviously doesn't believe that, and neither does Selena."

Edmund shrugged and thrust both hands in the pockets of his slacks. "They'll both accept it in time," he predicted mildly.

"Perhaps even faster," Emily replied, as the hurt and resentment inside her grew by leaps and bounds, "if you continue to make outrageous suggestions, like marrying me."

His eyes darkened, even as he continued to study her with the same unstoppable optimism and bemusement. "It wasn't exactly a suggestion," he told her.

"Oh, no?" Emily retorted smugly as he glided closer, not stopping until they stood toe-to-toe.

"It was a proposal."

"Really," Emily replied dryly, deciding then and there that Edmund Fairfax was one very exasperating, and very attractive, man. Kind and considerate one minute, unbearably autocratic and single-minded the next. The woman who married him would find her life anything but dull.

"Yes," Edmund responded in kind. "And if you'll listen to me with an open mind," he said as he took her hands in his, in a manner Emily found all the more presumptuous, "you'll understand why marriage is the answer to all our problems."

UNFORTUNATELY, Edmund thought, so far Emily wasn't buying into the idea. She slipped her hands from his, but kept her eyes on his. "I'm listening," she said quietly.

"You and Bobby need protection from your in-laws. The Bancrofts have power and influence in Maryland. The Fairfaxes have both in abundance in Kentucky. You alone against the Bancrofts would be an unfair fight, one you're so sure you have no hope of winning you've fled the state. But pit me and Gail—who's one heck an attorney—with you against the Bancrofts, and you begin to have a chance. But you still need an edge to ensure you'll win."

"And that edge is marriage," Emily assumed slowly, her expression softening.

"And the formation of a solid family unit," Edmund emphasized. Aware much was riding on this—for both of them—he edged closer. "You said it yourself. Bobby and Chloe get along great."

Emily lifted her head. It was easy to see she wanted to join forces with him, she just didn't think it would be that easy to defeat the combination of family and social pressures working against both of them. Her sea blue eyes glimmering with mistrust, she pressed her lips together mutinously. "Bobby and Chloe barely know each other."

"But already the connection is there. They need siblings. This is a chance—maybe even the only chance—they may have to actually have one."

Emily regarded him impatiently. "What are you going to get out of this?"

"A normal life. A relief from this constant matchmaking of my mother's. She thinks I need to be married. And—" Edmund shrugged, thinking of his immediate, physical reaction to Emily that afternoon, and again that evening "—maybe she's right."

Maybe I shouldn't rule out having a woman in my life again—though in a very different way.

"There's only one problem with this proposal, Edmund. I'm not interested in having a romantic relationship with anyone else," Emily interrupted. More softly she added, "I don't know if I have any love left to give to another man."

"I know what you mean," Edmund said, aware that he did not want her to leave. Not today. Not tomorrow. Not ever. "What I'm asking for here is a platonic relationship. A friendship. A support system, for both of us, and our kids."

"Or in other words, a marriage of convenience with no sex and no romance." Emily said with more verve.

Edmund paused, letting his eyes trail over her from head to toe. He had an idea what she wanted to hear from him on that score, but he respected her too much to be anything less than forthright. "I agree we shouldn't rush things or put undue pressure on ourselves to make something…erotic happen," Edmund told her practically as hot, embarrassed color swept her cheeks. "But at the same time, I don't want to arbitrarily rule anything out should we ever get to the point where our inclinations *are* aroused."

Emily's chin shot up another notch. She studied the way he stood, arms folded in front of him, legs braced apart, then slowly shook her head in mute astonishment. "I don't believe you," she said hotly.

"Why?" Edmund asked just as bluntly, not about to back down now. "Because I'm honest enough, and farsighted enough, to admit there might be a time somewhere down the road when we might change our minds and decide neither of us were meant to live like monks?''

Emily's eyes widened and her soft, bow-shaped lips parted in a round O of surprise. "You mean that, don't you?" she gasped.

Edmund shrugged, not about to start pulling any punches now, when he was so close to having her in his corner, and in his life. "I like to keep my options open," he said meaningfully, knowing it was a rule that had served him well. "So should you."

Emily's eyes gleamed with a mutinous light—as if she knew this was an argument, at least on principle, that she just wouldn't win.

Her mouth snapped shut. "Fine," she countered briskly, regarding him hotly, her breasts rising and falling with each highly agitated breath, "but if we ever got to that point—and mind you, I'm not in any way promising we would, no matter how young we are or how long or intimately we're together!—I want the option to nix it in the bud."

That, Edmund had no problem agreeing with. He had no desire for anything lackluster in that department, either. "You've got it."

Was she nuts to actually be considering this? Emily wondered, as a contemplative silence fell between them.

What Edmund was offering her was unusual, certainly. And yet there had been many times over the past year when she had wanted nothing more than to be able to give Bobby a loving father. Edmund felt the same about giving Chloe a mother. If they worked together, they would be able to provide a warm and nurturing two-parent home, plus a sibling for their children. That was one step better than the conditions she'd already been eager to accept, coming into the situation as Chloe's live-in nanny. And, she was eager for change.

Life had been bleak this last year. Yet, since corresponding with Edmund—in writing at first—then talking to him on the phone, and finally seeing him, she'd begun to feel alive again. She'd begun to feel like taking charge of her life. She didn't want that feeling to go away any more than she wanted to live a life on the run.

"Look, I know all this—" Edmund gestured at the grand mansion around them "—can be intimidating—"

"Actually, it's a lot like my former in-laws' home," Emily murmured. Only warmer, somehow. Less exclusive. More…intimate.

"But we're nothing like your in-laws."

That Emily was not so sure about. In certain respects, they were exactly the same. "Your mother—"

"Is full of bluster as usual, but in the end, she only wants Chloe's and my happiness. When she sees you—and Bobby—are the key to that, she'll come around, more quickly than you can imagine," Edmund said with assurance.

Emily glanced up at the ruggedly handsome contours of his face, appreciating his warmth and his strength. She enjoyed being on her own. She would also enjoy having someone in her life she could lean on again, whenever the need arose. Thoughtfully, she bit her lower lip, sighed. "There's no doubt it would be helpful to me to have you on my side in the upcoming custody fight with my in-laws."

"So what do you say?" Edmund prodded with an unrepentant grin.

Emily took a deep breath. "All right, I'll agree to it," she said. *But only as long as it's a marriage in name only.*

SECONDS LATER, there was a rap on the library door. Edmund opened it and Gail breezed in. "Mother sent me in here to talk some sense into you two."

"Too late," Edmund grinned as he laced a proprietorial arm about Emily's waist and tugged her close to his side. "She's agreed."

Gail surveyed them both in stunned amazement. "You two are nuts," she said flatly.

"Maybe," Edmund agreed with a smile.

"What's really going on here?" Gail demanded, placing both hands on her hips.

Edmund studied his younger sister with an unreadable look, as Emily felt herself turning an embarrassing shade of pink. "Exactly what you think," he said blandly. "An elopement."

Gail glanced out the windows, where the snow was still pounding them with bucket upon bucket of snow. "You're not going out in this weather!" she exclaimed.

Edmund regarded his younger sister smugly, even as he guided Emily to the sofa, where they both took a seat. "Fortunately, we don't have to," he said.

Gail blinked in astonishment, then threw up her hands. "Oh, no—"

"You owe me, Gail," Edmund persisted, sitting so close to Emily she could feel the heat of his thigh through the wool of his trousers and the satin fabric of her skirt.

Gail flung herself into a wing chair opposite them. "I can't marry you."

"Sure you can," Edmund insisted cheerfully as he draped an arm across Emily's shoulders. "You moonlight weekends as a justice of the peace at the Sweet Briar Chapel of Love."

"True enough," Gail replied, just as blithely, "but I can't issue a license."

"No, but you can make a few phone calls, call in a few markers and expedite the issuance of one," Edmund said.

"There's a three-day waiting period in this state—" Gail reminded.

"And a special statute in this particular county," Edmund responded, "that allows JPs to waive that waiting period, at their own discretion, if sufficient reason exists."

"And what reason would that be?" Gail asked, with a lively toss of her head.

Edmund draped an arm across her shoulders. "Let's just say Emily and I don't have any time to waste."

Gail gave Emily a pointed look. "Do you feel this way, too?"

With the Bancrofts and a host of private detectives on her tail right now? Emily drew a deep breath and tried not to tremble at his touch. *In for a penny, in for a pound. And she had said yes to his proposal.* "I think at this point an elopement is just what I—we—need," Emily said firmly. *Before I change my mind and chicken out.*

Gail studied them in thoughtful silence. "What about blood tests?" she asked quietly. Beginning, Emily thought, to see how serious this was.

Edmund smiled, relieved. "We've both had physicals in the last month, with complete blood tests."

Emily remembered. Edmund had said it wasn't necessary, but she'd been due for her yearly checkup anyway, and had figured it only fair of her to pass the results of her medical examination on, as part of the preemployment process.

"As a matter of fact—" Edmund unwreathed his arm from her shoulders, vaulted to his feet, went to the desk and unlocked the bottom drawer "—I've got both records right here."

He handed them over and waited patiently while Gail perused them quickly. "You seem to have thought of everything," Edmund's sister said finally. "Except one thing." She looked up expectantly. "What are you going to tell Chloe?"

"YOU MEAN YOU'RE going to be my mommy and not just my nanny?" Chloe said, delighted, when Edmund and Emily had finished telling her of their plans.

"Yes, if that's okay with you," Emily said, smiling.

"And then Bobby will be my brother?"

Edmund nodded at his daughter. "Right."

"Cool!" Chloe launched herself into Emily's arms and gave her a hug. "I always wanted a baby brother!" Still beaming, Chloe also gave Edmund a hug, then turned to Bobby, who was busy watching all the commotion with wide, blue eyes. "Did you hear that, Bobby?" she exclaimed gleefully, giving him a hug, too, as he let out another string of baby talk. "We're gonna be brother and sister!"

Bobby grabbed hold of a tyke-size plastic picnic table and pulled himself to a standing position. Grinning proudly, he picked up one foot, then the other, and walked back and forth alongside the table, using both hands to steady himself all the while.

"Wow, Daddy, did you see that?" Chloe said. "He's almost walking by himself."

Grinning, Bobby turned to face Emily. Ever so slowly and cautiously, he let go of the table. Knowing he was going to try to walk to her, she held out her hands to him. But Bobby pushed her hands away, and faced Edmund instead. Yelling something that sounded like "rabby-hata," whatever that meant, he bounced up and down slightly, as if he were raring to go.

"C'mon, bucko, you can do it," Edmund encouraged, holding out his hands, too. Again, Bobby waved away the offer of assistance with a frustrated scowl. He bounced harder but still did not pick up his feet. The extra effort left him off balance. He pitched forward awkwardly, dropped to his hands and knees. After a moment of confusion, he looked up at them with a silly grin. They all laughed at his clowning around and went back to their conversation.

"So when's the wedding?" Chloe asked Edmund, as Bobby crawled onto Emily's lap and cuddled contentedly.

Gail came in the nursery and gave Edmund the thumbs-up sign.

Edmund smiled. He bent to kiss his daughter's cheek, and then his "son's." "Tonight."

"YOU'RE REALLY going through with this?" Maureen asked with a skeptical look as Edmund and Emily, Gail and the kids, and every member of the household staff who was present that evening gathered in the living room.

"Yes. We most certainly are," Edmund murmured as he left Emily and the children and crossed to his mother's and Selena's sides. "And we'd like you both to stay. But only—" he cautioned wryly, in an aside only his mother and the woman she wanted him to marry could hear "—if we can count on you to behave."

"Actually," Selena said dryly, giving Edmund a glittering, unrequited look as she crossed her arms in front of her, "I wouldn't miss it for the world. I'm sure," Selena continued quietly, her glance raking over Emily's brocade satin evening suit, and the hastily assembled flowers snatched from existing household floral arrangements that were serving as her wedding bouquet, "the entire county is going to be talking about this insanity for weeks."

Refusing to let them spoil what was quickly becoming one of the most memorable evenings of his life, Edmund grinned and teased, "Then it's a good thing you're here, so you and Mother can give them all the details."

Maureen grimaced in a beleaguered manner. "You think this is amusing now, son," she hissed, "but mark my words. I guarantee you there will come a time when you will not only rue your hasty actions, but will no longer see the humor in all this, either. And when that day comes—"

"You'll be here to say 'I told you so,' I know," Edmund interrupted, rolling his eyes.

"And I," Selena murmured loftily, undaunted in her appreciation of him, "will be here to help you pick up the pieces."

Even if I don't want you to be? Edmund thought, wondering what in the world it would take to discourage the voracious socialite. Heaven knew it wasn't in his nature to be cruel to anyone—generally he felt there were much better ways to handle even the most disturbing situations—but Selena tempted him to be brutal.

Gail interrupted the tête-à-tête by motioning them over. She inclined her head at Bobby, who was yawning sleepily in Mrs. Hamilton's arms.

"I think we'd better get started," Gail said.

"We are assembled here to gather Emily and Edmund in the honorable estate of marriage. Those who enter this relationship are admonished to treat each other with mutual esteem and love...to bear with each other's infirmities and weaknesses...to comfort each other in sickness, trouble and sorrow...and to provide for each other, and for their household, in temporal things...and to live together, as the heirs of the grace of life."

While Emily trembled and Edmund's heart raced, Gail paused, her expression sober and intent.

"Edmund and Emily, is it your intention to share with each other your joys and sorrows and all that the years will bring, and with your promises here tonight, bind yourselves to each other as husband and wife?"

Edmund looked deep into Emily's eyes. She looked deep into his. A rush of satisfaction went through him. He knew they were doing this primarily for their kids, but standing here with Emily, actually getting married to each other, it was hard to remember this marriage was going to be one in name only. Nevertheless, the vows they were taking were serious, and they'd made certain with Gail beforehand that they were vows the two of them could keep.

"It is," Edmund and Emily said in unison.

"Then I ask you to join right hands." Gail waited while they did so.

"Repeat after me...I, Edmund, take you Emily to be my wife from this day forward...to join with you and your child, and together, share all that is to come...."

Hope for the future swept through him. In a voice that was husky with emotion, Edmund repeated the vows. Emily did the same. To his surprise, her voice was just as filled with emotion and promise as his, while around them the staff both smiled and wept, and Selena and Maureen looked on in shock.

"By the power and authority vested in me, I now pronounce you man and wife," Gail said, grinning at them both. "Edmund, you may kiss the bride."

Oh no, Emily thought. No. But it was too late. Her new husband had already taken her masterfully in his warm, strong arms. His dark eyes glittering with desire, he deliberately lowered his lips to hers, and bestowed upon her a sweet and tender kiss. In reality, the sizzling caress couldn't have lasted more than five seconds, but the impact on Emily was unmistakable. Her breath stalled in her chest, her heart slammed against her ribs and she went perilously weak in the knees. The instinct and yearning within her took over. The next thing she knew she had dropped the bouquet and wreathed her arms around his neck, and was kissing him back, just as sweetly, just as tenderly, just as meaningfully. For this was the beginning of the promise they had made to each other, the promise they meant with all their hearts and souls to keep. This was the way they would give their children—and each other—the complete family that had been denied them.

Slowly, they'd come together. Slowly, they drew apart. Emily gazed up at Edmund. Edmund gazed down at her. And in that instant, as their eyes met and held, she knew he was just as affected, just as stunned, by the electricity flowing between them as she. Suddenly, nothing was as simple as it had seemed. Nor, Emily worried, would it ever be again.

Only the sound of Chloe's melodic little voice brought them back to reality. "Daddy?" Chloe asked, still looking a little starry-eyed by all that had happened that evening. "Do we get to have a wedding cake…?"

Reluctantly, Edmund let go of Emily, turned to face his daughter, and knelt down beside her. "No, pumpkin, not tonight. It's pretty late." He glanced out the window, and saw—as did Emily and everyone else—that the snow was coming down very hard now, in thick white sheets. "I think we're just going to go back to the cottage."

"But we will get one soon?" Chloe persisted.

If it meant that much to her? Emily and Edmund nodded in unison. "We certainly will," Edmund promised.

Anxious to get his family home, Edmund called down to the barns and had one of the hired hands use a farm tractor to scoop the fast-accumulating snow off the driveway between the main house and the cottage. Nevertheless, visibility was so poor, the snow coming down so hard by then, that the three-minute drive back to the cottage took ten.

And that was long enough for the evening to catch up with them. By the time they had both children inside and in their pajamas, Chloe and Bobby were both yawning mightily. Five minutes later, Emily noted, both were asleep. And then it was just the two of them, Edmund and Emily, alone.

Chapter Four

"Amazing, how quiet it is, isn't it?" Emily said awkwardly at last as she finished preparing Bobby's baby bottles of milk and juice for the next day, and then put them in the refrigerator.

Edmund nodded as the two of them kicked off their shoes and settled side by side on the sofa before the fireplace. "I feel that way every evening after Chloe goes to sleep," he confided.

Trying hard not to be affected by the sudden intimacy of the situation, or the crisp wintry scent of his cologne, Emily turned to face him. "What's Chloe's usual bedtime?"

"In the short time since we've been back to Kentucky, I haven't really kept to any particular routine, much to my mother's dismay. But back in Seattle, it's eight-thirty on school nights. Weekends there, I let her stay up until nine. What's Bobby's bedtime?"

Emily smiled, glad Edmund was as flexible and relaxed a parent as she was. "It depends. Usually around seven-thirty or eight."

Edmund continued to survey her thoughtfully. With his jacket off and tie loosened, the first two buttons on his shirt undone, he radiated all the male power and casual sexiness of a big screen hero. Unbidden, all sorts of romantic thoughts and fantasies came to mind. Emily pushed them away. "Does Bobby sleep through the night?" Edmund asked.

Emily felt herself flush with an inner warmth she could not contain. "Yes," she answered casually, dropping her glance to the strong column of his throat, and the crisp curling hair visible in the open V of his shirt, "unless he's sick or teething. He has for quite a while now."

Edmund nodded. Aware they'd exhausted the subject of bedtimes, a silence fell between them that was even more awkward. What were they going to do with all the long evenings ahead of them? Emily wondered, realizing all over again just how handsome and physically appealing her new husband was. She hadn't considered that at the time she'd agreed to their hasty marriage.

She hadn't considered the sheer chemistry between them, either. She'd thought a marriage of convenience was all she wanted, until she found herself in his arms and looked into his eyes and experienced the overwhelming sexiness of his kiss, and then she'd known; the physical side of her...the side of her that still longed to be kissed and held and touched—the part of her that still yearned to be wanted and loved— wasn't dead after all.

He quirked a brow at the increasingly pink contours of her face. "Something bothering you?" he asked, concerned.

Yes, as a matter of fact, Emily thought, aware being in such close proximity to him had left her feeling unaccountably jittery and excited inside. Unless she got hold of herself, and put those feelings aside, who knew what might happen between them on this—their official wedding night? Especially with the blizzard raging outside, a fire roaring inside, and both children sound asleep? They were vulnerable here. Both of them. She had to remember that. "Um, listen, Edmund," she began casually, turning to him, her bent knee accidentally brushing his thigh. "About that kiss back at the house—" Emily said, as she shifted backward ever so slightly. Heat centered in her chest, then began to move outward in radiating waves.

Edmund smiled. "I caught you off guard with that, I know."

And how! She'd never felt such sizzle. "You certainly did," Emily retorted dryly, pretending she was experienced enough to have not given it a second thought.

Edmund gave her the slow, thoughtful once-over. "I decided it should look as real as possible."

What did he mean look? Emily wondered. She swallowed around the sudden constriction in her throat and struggled to get air into her lungs. "You were acting?"

He shrugged his broad shoulders in matter-of-fact admission. "Out of duty. At least it started that way."

"And then—?" she said, aware her heart was slamming against her ribs.

"Then, much to my surprise," Edmund said softly as he reached up to stroke her cheekbone with his thumb. He favored her with a slow, sensual smile. "I got into it. As did you."

Emily blushed fiercely and drew away. "Like you said," she murmured, smoothing the tousled hair from her face, "I thought it should look good."

Arms folded in front of him, he leaned close, his eyes twinkling. "I think we fooled them all right."

Emily's face grew even warmer as she thought about the potential ramifications of what they'd done, kissing that way. Like it or not, in the few hours since she'd been with Edmund, she'd felt...something. Not lust, actually, and certainly not love, but something. Some physical attraction. Some...magic. Worse, she now worried that their earlier agreement to maintain an emotionally warm and supportive but currently platonic arrangement was already in jeopardy, after just a few hours! Edmund had talked about facing the issue of a sexual relationship much further down the road. He had acted as if they could handle that if and when it ever came up, probably by making love as "friends" who also happened to be "man and wife."

Yet for her, that part of her life was already changing...in a manner that was far too fast, and far too overpowering, for comfort. And that being the case, there was only one sensible way to proceed.

"Edmund?" Emily said, knotting her damp hands in front of her and briefly closing her eyes.

"Hm?" he asked in a soft, victorious voice that sent shivers of awareness racing over her skin.

Emily took a bracing breath and opened her eyes. She was determined to deal with this situation logically. "I think in the future we ought to curtail any expected displays of affection to token hugs, and whenever possible avoid kissing altogether."

Edmund grinned. He took her hand and lifted it to his lips. "I agree, I don't want to be kissing you for anyone else's benefit but mine."

Emily wrung her hand from his. "That's *not* what I meant," she reprimanded.

"I know."

Couldn't he see she was trying to keep them both from getting hurt? "You can't honestly be thinking about kissing me again?" Emily scolded as her temper flared.

"Just for the benefit of my mother and Selena? Hell, no. If I kiss you again," he said softly, meaningfully as his gaze slid over her in a sensual, unmistakable way, "it's going to be for me."

As Edmund had expected, Emily looked shocked by his pronouncement.

She recovered quickly. "But we both know you're not going to kiss me again," Emily reiterated stubbornly, "since it was only *required* during the actual marriage ceremony."

"And actually not even then," Edmund stated casually, aware her expression had grown stony with resolve. "We could have refused the opportunity to lock lips."

"But that would've aroused suspicion," Emily conceded dryly, the first hint of humor curving her soft, bow-shaped lips.

"Right," Edmund agreed, studying his new marriage partner with great care.

"And suspicion we didn't—don't—need," Emily said reasonably, her spirits picking up with every second that passed.

"I think we have enough to deal with, without having others suspect our motives"

"Which, unfortunately, they already do."

True enough, Edmund thought, as he took her hand in his and held it. "They'll get over it quickly when they see how happy the children are, and what a good family the four of us make," he predicted confidently.

Emily studied the fit of her hand in his. "I guess you're right," she murmured softly.

But as for the rest, Edmund thought... A marriage in name only had seemed like a good idea until he had kissed her and held her in his arms. Oh, he'd known from the moment she walked into his cottage that afternoon that he could still find a woman physically attractive. Just being around her had sent all his senses into overdrive.

What he hadn't realized, until the moment he'd taken her in his arms—despite all his lighthearted teasing to the contrary—was that he could still feel the white-hot lightning bolt of desire. Or that the need to hold her and have her would hit him like a ton of bricks the moment his lips touched hers.

Despite their pretending it was so, that hadn't been an ordinary kiss they'd shared, any more than theirs was an ordinary marriage. He sensed if and when they ever kissed again, there'd be nothing dull or ordinary about it.

If they ever kissed.

Right now, he realized, stunned by the sharpness of his disappointment, she didn't look as if she thought that would be a good idea.

Considering the ardent nature of his feelings, and her lack of reserve in return, he had to admit hers was a more cautious, and much more practical, attitude.

It still left him feeling oddly bereft and in some ways, more acutely lonely than before.

She looked down at her bare left hand that should have held a wedding band, proclaiming her as his bride.

Edmund frowned, unhappy there'd been no time to get wedding bands for both of them. "I'll call the jeweler in the morning and get some wedding rings sent out to the house as soon as the weather permits."

Emily blinked and looked distracted—as if wedding rings and blizzards were the last thing on her mind. "That's fine," she said gently.

"Well..." It was either end the cozy evening now, or risk kissing her again. Edmund released his hold on her hand and stood. He forced himself to contain his reluctance to leave her side. "I guess we should say good-night—the kids are going to be up early."

"You're right," Emily said, smiling. She took the hand he offered and stood in a drift of flowery perfume. "They are."

Together, they turned out the lights and walked toward the hall. She turned to go into her bedroom. He turned to go into his. Her hand still on the doorknob, she turned back, her lovely face gilded in reflected light and shadow. "Edmund?" she murmured softly, so as not to wake the kids.

He trod closer. And said, just as quietly, "Yes?"

Tilting her head back, so she could more easily see into his face, she searched his eyes. "Do you have any regrets about what we did tonight—about getting married the way we did?"

Only one, that I won't be making love to you tonight, Edmund thought. Edmund looked down at her, shook his head, and said in all honesty, "Not a one."

"Up!" BOBBY DEMANDED early the next morning as he stood gripping the railing on his crib. "Up!"

Emily plucked a diaper out of the bag and hurried to get him before his exuberant demands woke Chloe and Edmund.

"Bah-dell."

"We'll get your bottle, sweetheart," Emily soothed. "Let's get you dry first, okay?"

Bobby grinned as she put the railing down and placed him on his back. "Hi," he said, waving at her and kicking both feet.

"Hi, yourself." Emily grinned back at her son as she unsnapped his pajamas and removed the damp diaper. "Did you have a good night's sleep? I sure did." Better than she'd had in months. Maybe because she felt so safe and happy here with Edmund, as if as long as she and Bobby were here with him and Chloe everything was going to be all right.

"But then," Emily told her son, "it's been a pretty eventful few days." And the next, as she and Edmund settled into marriage, would be all the more eventful, she was sure.

Bobby chatted nonstop as she sprinkled powder on his bottom and finished changing him. "Bah-dell!" he demanded as she fastened him into fresh clothing and picked him up in her arms. "Bah-dell, bah-dell!"

"All right, sweetie, we'll go get your bah-dell right now, just calm down a moment," Emily murmured as she rushed out the bedroom door and ran smack into Edmund's chest.

He was clad in a plain white T-shirt that clung to the defined muscles of his shoulders, chest, and washboard-flat abs. Soft, faded gray cotton sweatpants did equally impressive things for his hips and thighs. Like her, it was obvious he had just awakened. His dark brown hair was rumpled, his sable brown eyes soft and sleepy, his face lined with morning beard.

Emily tried not to inhale the wintry scent of cologne clinging to skin, or notice the sexy peppering of morning beard on his handsome face. "I didn't know you were out here."

"So I see," Edmund teased as his eyes swept her from head to foot, taking in her sleep-flushed cheeks and tousled hair, then moving to her pink flannel pajamas and matching flannel robe. Fires of awareness ignited over every securely clad inch of her as he pushed the rumpled hair off his forehead with the flat of his hand and confided in a husky tenor, "I was trying to be quiet so I wouldn't wake you."

They were married, living together under one roof. They'd have to get used to this, Emily schooled herself sternly, even as her pulse picked up another notch.

"Too late," she said blithely, in response to his remark about waking her. "Bobby already woke me." And if he hadn't, the sight of Edmund, thusly clad, sure would've. He looked sexy and scrumptious enough to appear in a men's underwear ad.

Edmund grinned and fell in step beside her as she headed for the kitchen, a still-chanting Bobby braced on her hip. "When did you get up?"

"About five minutes ago." Emily pulled a bottle of milk from the fridge, and pulled out a pan in which to warm it. "You?"

"The same." Edmund reached past her to turn on the warm water in the faucet. "Chloe wanted me to see the snow."

Emily set Bobby's bottle in a pan of warm water. "Did we get a lot?" Emily hadn't yet had the opportunity to look.

Edmund grinned and beckoned her and Bobby closer. "Come see for yourself."

Emily moved to his side. Together, they stared out

the window at a veritable winter wonderland. A thick white layer of snow covered the ground and draped the trees. Farm buildings were coated with white. And more snow was still coming down. "There must be a foot out there!" Emily exclaimed.

Edmund pointed to the snow piled up along the pasture fence. "At least. Plus drifts of up to two feet."

Bobby touched his hand to the glass. He pressed his face forward, a perplexed look on his face.

"Has he seen snow before this?" Edmund asked gently, grinning at the incredulity on Bobby's face.

"Not that he'd remember," Emily said softly, as she cradled her son in her arms. "We haven't had any yet this winter."

Chloe popped up beside them. "Can Bobby go out and play in the snow with us this morning?" Chloe asked. "We've got a baby sled he can sit in, that was mine when I was little, plus one for me!"

Emily studied the snow falling, which had now faded to a light but persistent precipitation. "I guess it will be all right, but just for a little while. And we all will have to dress very warmly—and that means boots, hats, mittens, long underwear, everything!"

"Can Daddy come, too?" Chloe asked both adults simultaneously.

Their glances met above her head. "Sure," Edmund said. "Why not? Sounds like fun."

"Hurrah!" Elated, Chloe did a little dance.

"We all have to eat breakfast first, though," Edmund cautioned. "And Emily and I need time to drink some coffee."

Coffee, Emily thought, sounded heavenly.

"Okay, but can Bobby and I play while you grown-ups cook breakfast? I got his toys out. And some of my stuffed animals.''

"That'll be fine,'' Emily said. "Just let me get his bottle for him.''

Minutes later, Bobby and Chloe were both sitting on the floor, playing with the pull-apart blocks, and Edmund and Emily were in the kitchen, making breakfast when the telephone rang. Edmund switched on the coffeemaker with one hand, reached for the telephone with the other. "Edmund Fairfax— Hi, yes, we were expecting you. I understand. The weather— We'll reschedule.'' He paused, frowning. "I see. There isn't anything I can say to change your mind? Right.'' He hung up, his jaw set.

The look on his face had her heart going out to him. "Bad news?'' Emily asked as she lifted sizzling strips of bacon from the skillet and put them on paper toweling to drain.

"Very.'' Edmund grimaced as he, too, headed back to the stove. "Another customer just canceled his appointment to have his champion mare bred and foaled at Fairfax Farm.''

Emily wanted to understand and be supportive, as his wife, and as his friend. To do that she'd have to get him talking. "Does this happen often?'' she asked gently.

Edmund shook his head, his expression upset. "When my father was running the farm, we always had a waiting list.''

"And now?''

"This year—'' Edmund sighed unhappily "—we'll be lucky if we make it through the breeding season with all the slots filled.''

Emily added bread to the toaster while Edmund

scrambled the eggs with an expert hand. "When is the breeding season?"

"It runs from February to June," Edmund answered, distracted.

"And people bring their horses here to have their foals sired by one of your stallions."

"Right. Then, because we have a vet here to look after them, and top-notch facilities for birthing, most of the horses stay on during gestation."

Emily carried butter and jelly to the table, then returned to his side. "Which—in horses—is how long?"

"Approximately three hundred thirty-seven days or eleven months."

Emily smiled, enjoying the winter, but also anticipating the spring. "It must be pretty exciting around here, when all the foals are being born."

"It is." Edmund's expression turned determined as he moved the eggs into a serving dish. "And it'll be even more exciting if King's Ransom, last year's Kentucky Derby winner, is turned out to stud here. Just having a horse of that caliber here will bring in tons of business. And perhaps make clients like the Thurstons change their minds about taking their long-standing business contracts from us, too."

"That's a possibility?" Emily asked, plucking the last of the toast from the toaster.

"Very much so," Edmund confirmed. "I've been talking to Mr. and Mrs. King—the owners of the stallion—every day since I've been back."

"When will you know if that's going to happen?" Emily asked curiously as they carried the steaming dishes of food to the table.

"Hopefully, by the end of the week. Mr. and Mrs.

King are still fielding offers from other horse farms in the area, but they said they'll make a decision by then."

"I hope you get the business," Emily said.

Edmund's eyes met hers in a way that made her feel they were really partners. "So do I."

"Daddy, Emily, come quick!" Chloe said. "You've got to look at the TV!"

"What is it?" Edmund said, already heading that way. Emily was right beside him.

"They're going to show pictures of people who got lost in the blizzard after the commercial!" Chloe continued enthusiastically.

"See?" Chloe pointed at the television screen.

The male newscaster announced cheerfully, "First up is a photo of Nora Hart Kingsley—a runaway bride-to-be from Pittsburgh, Pennsylvania. She apparently got cold feet and left the church shortly before her wedding. She hasn't been heard of since the blizzard began and those who know her speculate she might still be in her wedding gown. Her father, Charles Kingsley, is offering a reward for any information on her whereabouts."

The female newscaster said, "And I heard her fiancé was frantic, too."

"As he might well be," acknowledged her cohost.

"Next up is a story about a schoolteacher from The Peach Blossom Academy for Young Women in Arlington, Virginia." Photos of a pretty blond woman and seven adorable little girls in private school uniform flashed on the screen. "Grace Tennessen was on a history field trip with seven of her students in rural Virginia. The headmistress of the Academy was frantic when they didn't make it to their scheduled destination. Considering the ferocity of the blizzard in the mountains—they got something like two feet of snow last night with drifts up to three and four feet!—it's no wonder everyone was frightened for them, but apparently they're all okay." The female newscaster smiled slyly, then continued in a speculation-filled tone, "They've taken shelter with what our sources in Blue Mountain Gap, Virginia, tell us is a very handsome and sought after young bachelor."

The male cohost made a comical face. "Sounds promising," he said wryly. "And last but not least of our latest blizzard stories—" Two more photos flashed on the screen, big as life.

Edmund, Emily and Chloe all gasped in unison. Then Chloe pointed and exclaimed excitedly, "Look. It's Emily and baby Bobby! They're both on TV!"

Chapter Five

Emily stared at the photo of Bobby and herself flashing across the television set.

"The young widow and her son have been missing since early yesterday, and are feared lost in the storm," the announcer was saying. A photo of her station wagon and the license plate of her car flashed on the screen. "Please call the Maryland police or your local highway patrol with any information on their whereabouts."

"What are they talking about? You're not missing, Emily! And neither is Bobby! You're right here!" Chloe said happily as she grinned at Bobby and tucked her fingers into Emily's.

"But my in-laws don't know that," Emily murmured, thinking it was just like the well-connected Whit and Andrea Bancroft to sound an alarm heard nationwide before even a day had passed. More to the point, it was such a great human interest story— "Mother And Baby Lost In Record Blizzard!"—that it probably hadn't even been all that hard to get the national news show to pick up the story and run with it.

She could imagine what would come next. Their

photos would appear on the cover of some major newsmagazine. There'd be a story inside telling how distraught Emily had been since Brian's death, a little over a year before. Followed by the Bancrofts' tour de force appearances on "Oprah" and "Geraldo," complete with restrained but tearful pleas to return Bobby and her to their loving care. Before they knew it, Edmund and his family would find themselves sucked into the maelstrom of hurtful publicity and damaged reputations. Even if she followed her original plan and ran away again, there'd be no place in the country she could go to begin again, without fear of being recognized and turned in for some cash reward.

Edmund closed the distance between them with easy, sensual grace. "You're going to have to telephone them and tell them you've eloped."

Emily suppressed a heartfelt sigh and tried not to dread what was coming next. Feeling suddenly cold and unprotected, she tucked the lapels of her flannel bathrobe closer to her chest, and tightened the belt at her waist. "I know. I'll do it as soon as breakfast is over."

He covered her hands with his. "You can use the telephone in my bedroom, if you like."

Emily smiled up at him, taking strength in the knowledge whatever happened, he was there to stand beside her. "Thanks."

The four of them sat down and had breakfast together. As soon as the meal was over, the kids returned to the toys spread out over the living room floor. "I'll handle the dishes," Edmund said. "You go ahead and make the call."

Emily supposed he was right. There was no reason

to put it off any longer. It certainly wouldn't get any easier. She went into the bedroom and perched on the edge of his sleep-rumpled sheets. The dark green paisley sheets had long ago lost the warmth of his body. But the scent of him, so crisp and wintry and evocatively male, clung to the soft Egyptian cotton.

Her hand shaking, she dialed the number she now knew by heart. A number her husband had seldom called when he was alive. Andrea Bancroft answered on the first ring. Emily drew a bolstering breath. "Hello, Andrea, this is Emily."

"Emily!" Relief and excitement mingled in Andrea's voice. "Where are you?"

Briefly, Emily explained about the elopement. Her announcement was greeted with silence.

"That was rather sudden, wasn't it?" Andrea said finally.

Emily sidestepped her former mother-in-law's question and replied simply, "I've known Edmund for several years. Brian introduced us." The two men had attended prep school together in Virginia. Edmund had been like a big brother to Brian, and though their jobs kept them apart, the two men had continued their friendship via phone calls and E-mail messages until Brian's death. "He's helped me a lot since we lost Brian, more than I would've ever thought possible," Emily explained.

"So you thought you'd marry him, just like that?" Andrea snapped, upset.

"Andrea, please." Emily rubbed at the tension headache starting in her temples. "I don't think we should discuss this."

"You're right," Andrea bit back stonily, as possessive and smothering as ever. "Not over the phone, we shouldn't."

And not in court, either, Emily thought.

"Whit and I will be there directly," Andrea promised in a smooth, cultured tone. "Maybe it's not too late to have this travesty annulled."

Emily's hands tightened on the phone until her fingers turned white. With effort, she spoke in a calm, even tone, "That is not your decision to make, Andrea."

There was a shuffling sound on the other end of the phone line. Sounds of whispering. Abruptly, Whit got on the phone. He had always been the more politic of the two, and this was no exception. "You're exhausted, Em. Overwhelmed. Getting caught out in this blizzard has no doubt upset you. But not to worry. It's not too late to undo anything you may have rushed into under duress. The courts will understand you've been under a tremendous strain the past year. We all have. Just know we're here to help you. And we'll be there as soon as we can." Giving her no chance to dissent further, Whit hung up.

As always, when confronted with her in-laws, Emily felt as if she'd been run over by a steamroller.

"Well, how'd it go?" Edmund asked when she returned to the kitchen where he was finishing up the last of the breakfast dishes.

Exactly as I figured, Emily thought. They refused to see the world through anyone's eyes but their own. "Badly," she murmured, loud enough so only he could hear. She leaned against the counter and folded her arms in front of her. "Whit and Andrea Bancroft see our elopement as further proof of my instability."

And she had to admit, given the quickness with

which she'd entered into said union, the Bancrofts may have had a point. No sane woman would have married a man she barely knew, no matter what his relationship to her deceased husband, or how sympatico they'd found themselves of late.

"Did Brian's parents threaten you?" Edmund asked, his sensual lips narrowing suspiciously as he closed the distance between them even more.

Not overtly, but then, that was as expected, too. Whit and Andrea excelled at subtle instigation and behind-the-scene machinations. Emily turned her gaze to his. "They said they were coming here, as soon as the weather permitted."

Seeing that bit of news as a reprieve, Edmund's broad shoulders relaxed beneath the soft fabric of his T-shirt. "It'll be days before the roads are cleared."

Days in which Whit and Andrea could come up with a strategy of their own. Emily bit into her lower lip worriedly as she turned her attention to the snow still drifting down in gentle white sprinkles. "They won't wait for that," Emily predicted grimly. Though she wished they would. She needed time to prepare. "They have their own jet."

Edmund's eyes veered to hers, and stayed. "So as soon as the airports in Maryland and Kentucky are open—"

"They'll be here," Emily said bluntly.

His eyes still on hers, he shrugged and picked up his coffee mug. He took a deep draught of steaming black coffee. "That still gives us at least a day or two."

And then what? Emily wondered nervously. When the Bancrofts showed up, would all hell break loose? Or would it be a much more discriminating form of browbeating and blackmailing going on? Would they attack just her, or Edmund and his family, too? "I hate bringing all this on to you and Chloe," she said softly, with genuine regret. Because however the Bancrofts managed to insinuate themselves into the situation, it would definitely be an uncomfortable, unpleasant experience.

"Hey." Edmund put his mug aside. He took both her hands in his and tugged her close. "We're in this together, remember?" he reminded her gruffly as his hands warmly and protectively clasped hers.

"I know, but—"

"No qualifiers." Lifting a hand to her face, he tucked a strand of hair behind her ear, then curved his hand against the underside of her chin, tipping her face up to his. "We promised to help each other last night, for better for worse, and we will," he said softly.

Emily knew that. And she wanted that.

She was also afraid they were on the verge of a complete disaster that had little or nothing to do with the blizzard that had kept her there in the first place.

"In the meantime," Edmund said gently, loosely wreathing an arm about her slender shoulders as he tucked her beneath the curve of his arm against his side. "I suggest we fight fire with fire."

Emily, who hadn't allowed herself the luxury of leaning on anyone in recent months, let herself melt into his warm, sustaining strength. "And how, pray tell, do we do that?" she quipped, laying her head on his shoulder and savoring his closeness despite herself.

Edmund grinned as if he were glad she had asked. "We call in a private investigator to dig up dirt on the Bancrofts,'' he said. ''Ten to one, there are reasons why they shouldn't have custody of Bobby, either. We just have to find out what those reasons are, and be prepared to use them.''

''Even in open court?'' she challenged, wondering just how far he was prepared to go.

''If it gets to that point,'' Edmund asserted grimly, squeezing her hand, ''you bet.''

''CHLOE, ARE YOU about dressed?'' Edmund asked as he glanced at his watch. He was anxious to get up to the main house and work on farm business, and now that the farm crews had all the tractors out, clearing the farm roads of the drifting snow, it was going to be possible to get his Jeep up there.

Chloe opened her bedroom door and walked out into the hall, clad in wool slacks, shirt and sweater. ''I was—until my socks got all squishy.''

Edmund looked down at his daughter's feet, which were bare, then at the soggy argyle socks she held in her hand. His brows knit together as he asked, perplexed, ''Did you spill something?''

''No. It's the rug in my room, over by my closet. It's all wet, Daddy, *wet and cold.*''

This did not sound good. Edmund held out his hand to her. ''Show me.''

Chloe grabbed hold of him, marched him into her room and over to the far wall. ''See, here, Daddy? See how cold it is?''

Without warning, Emily appeared in the door, Bobby on her hip. They, too, were all dressed and ready to go. ''What's going on?''

Edmund felt the water seeping out from beneath the floorboard. *This was just what they needed, with*

*the snow still coming down, and the area hotels all
full with stranded travellers.* "Looks like a burst pipe.
I'm going to have to go outside and turn off the water."

"Oh, no. Are you going to be able to get it fixed?"

"My guess is not for a few days." He paused, letting his words sink in.

Looking calm but concerned, Emily lifted her
glance to his. Thankfully, she was not a woman who
let little things disturb her. "What will we do in the
meantime?" she asked.

"The only thing we can." Edmund grimaced and
sighed just thinking about it. "Move to the main
house."

As EXPECTED, Edmund's mother, Maureen, was delighted to have them under her roof. "We'll get you
settled right away," she promised, leading the way
upstairs to the west wing. "Edmund and Emily, we'll
put you in the center bedroom. Chloe can be in the
pink bedroom to the left, and Bobby can use the nursery to the right."

"Thanks. We can take it from here," Edmund told
his mother as he shifted the heavy suitcases in his
hands.

"Of course." Maureen backed out graciously.
"Chloe, darling, would you like to come with me?
We've got piping hot cinnamon rolls in the kitchen."

Chloe looked at Edmund for permission. "Is it
okay, Daddy?"

Edmund nodded.

"What about Bobby? Do you think he'd like to
come along?" Maureen asked, already holding out
her hands to him.

"I guess he would," Emily murmured, surprised but pleased, as Bobby went into Maureen's arms with a gurgle and grin.

"We'll be down to collect them as soon as we get settled up here," Edmund promised.

"Take your time." Maureen smiled, and looking as if she were in seventh heaven with two grandchildren to care for, disappeared with the children around the corner.

Edmund carried their bags into the bedroom and set them down. When he returned minutes later with the rest of their bags, Emily was still looking at the cozy double bed in the center of the room. He set the luggage down, out of the way, and then moved to her side. "Problem?" he asked softly.

She kept her glance averted. "There's only one bed here, Edmund," she murmured as twin spots of color crept into her face.

"I know." And it was all he could do to block the image of the two of them, their bodies scantily clad and intimately entwined, out of his mind. They weren't going to make love here. Or anywhere else. He had to remember that. But letting go of the possibility was something easier said than done.

Emily's hands trembled as she slipped them into the deep slash pockets of her pleated wool trousers. The movement pulled the fabric more snugly against the slender curves of her hips and waist. The edge of her teeth scraping the softness of her soft pink lower lip, Emily quipped lightly, "I suppose asking for separate bedrooms is out of the question."

Edmund didn't want to make her uncomfortable. Nor did he want to be foolish. And right now they had too many eyes upon them, watching their every newlywed move. He edged closer, gently circled her wrist and slipped her hand from her pocket, snugly into his. "There are other rooms available," he acknowledged softly.

Her hand curled securely into the warmth of his.

"But doing so would raise suspicions," she guessed.

"Definitely." Edmund paused again, enjoying the silky fall of her shoulder-length hair against the healthy glow of her golden skin. Aware they were getting used to touching each other this way, to behaving very much like a couple, he gazed into her deep sea blue eyes. "It's only for a few days."

Her thick black lashes, the same color as her straight glossy hair, lowered demurely. Looking as if she were trying hard not to worry, Emily released a beleaguered sigh. "Right."

Sensing she needed comfort now more than ever, Edmund rubbed a thumb along the satiny underside of her wrist. "We're both adults."

Emily drew a deep breath, nodded, and again averted her eyes. "Right again."

"We can handle it," Edmund assured.

"I know, but—" Her wrist still in his hand, Emily swiveled toward him, her breasts accidentally brushing against his arm. "I can't help but thinking we're fooling ourselves to think it's going to be that simple. You're a man. I'm a woman." And, Edmund thought, I want like hell to kiss you again. "Knowing what we've already agreed, sharing one set of covers is bound to be awkward and uncomfortable for both of us."

No kidding, Edmund thought. She moved away, yet the feel of her, so soft and warm and womanly, was like a lightning bolt of desire, arrowing straight to his groin. Edmund grimaced against his rising erection, even as he struggled to keep his mind on the discussion and give her the reassurance she needed. "We'll handle it," he assured her bluntly, shifting his fingers so they entwined even more intimately with hers. Even if it left him aching with unslaked desire for a week, they'd handle it.

"Handle what?" Without warning, Selena Somerset appeared at the bedroom door. She positioned her index finger on her chin and gloated knowingly at them both. "Don't tell me there's trouble between you two?" she prodded gleefully. "Already?"

Edmund had helped her. It was time, Emily thought, for her to help him. Holding their clasped hands in front of them, she slipped beneath the curve of his arm and slid her other arm around his waist. Resting her cheek against the solid warmth of Edmund's shoulder, Emily smiled at the Mrs. Edmund Fairfax wanna-be. "Not to worry, Selena. It's nothing we can't handle," Emily told Selena smoothly.

"Just a little weather-induced calamity," Edmund agreed, as he tucked her even closer against his side.

Selena's eyes frosted over. "So I heard. Edmund, your mother sent me up to tell you there are a number of business calls she'd like you to return this morning on behalf of the farm. The messages—including one from the Thurstons about the luncheon and tour here tomorrow—are downstairs on the desk in the study."

Edmund nodded politely. "Please let her know I'll be down in a moment."

"Will do." Selena's glance cut once more to Emily. Frowning, she turned on her heel and glided back down the hall, her backside swaying provocatively beneath her trim wool suit.

Once she'd disappeared from view, Emily breathed a sigh of relief. As did Edmund. As abruptly as she'd slid into his arms, he let her go. It was a thoughtful move that left Emily feeling oddly bereft. "Thanks for the quick thinking," Edmund said smoothly. "I think the show of wifely adoration did a lot to discourage Selena."

If only that was all it had done, Emily thought wryly, as she struggled to tame her racing heart and weak, wobbly knees. "Glad to be of assistance," Emily said huskily. Aware her throat had suddenly become unbearably dry and her fantasies were still running wild, Emily lifted her arm to check her watch. Bobby'd been with Maureen almost half an hour. It was time to remove herself from the heaven of Edmund's presence and come down to earth. "I better check on Bobby."

"No need," Maureen said, coming down the hall toward her, a sleeping Bobby cuddled contentedly in her arms. "I've got him right here. Poor little fella drifted off in his high chair."

"I'll help you get him settled in his crib," Emily said, dashing ahead into the adjacent nursery.

"And I'll attend to those calls," Edmund said, striding off determinedly in the other direction.

Maureen shifted Bobby gently in her arms. "He takes a morning nap, I gather?"

"He used to take one every day. Now, it depends on how tired he is," Emily explained as she quietly lowered the side of the crib. She kept her voice low enough to prevent waking Bobby as she took him from Maureen and settled him on his back in the comfy crib. "Yesterday was a very long day."

Maureen watched as Emily covered Bobby with his favorite blanket and tucked his teddy bear in beside him. Sure he was cozy, Emily raised the side of the crib, turned on the baby monitor, and took the receiver with her out into the hall. "Thank you for watching him."

Maureen ushered them both into the playroom across the hall. "No problem. I enjoyed it," Maureen said, as she motioned Emily to a seat on the padded windowseat. "He's a delightful child. But now that he is asleep, I wonder if the two of us might talk, woman to woman, as two people who care deeply about my son."

Uh-oh, Emily thought, here it comes. Not that she could blame Edmund's mother for being protective. If it were Bobby's heart and well-being in question, Emily knew she'd behave the same way.

Maureen's expression became one of concern. "I saw the bulletin on the morning news shows. I then made a few telephone calls to friends in Maryland. I know Whit and Andrea Bancroft have been trying to rob you of your son, Bobby, and I think it's terrible. No one has the right to take a baby from his mother, and it's clear Bobby adores you and belongs with you."

Emily swallowed. Maureen had done her homework. "Does this mean you approve of my marriage to your son?" she asked cautiously.

"In a word? No." Maureen smiled gently. "Although it explains why he acted as impetuously as he did last night. He's trying to protect you and your son."

"It's true," Emily said carefully. "He cares what happens to us." And for that she'd be eternally grateful.

Maureen nodded briskly. "I don't doubt that for a minute, dear. Nevertheless, I still think the only reason to marry someone is to be head over heels in love with them."

There had been a time when Emily had agreed with that. Now, she wasn't so sure. She only knew that their lives had changed course irreparably. To be able to go on, she and Edmund would have to change course, too. "Edmund and I both have already had the loves of our lives," she responded fiercely. Neither were expecting such passion to come again.

Maureen shook her head in a reproving manner. "It doesn't mean love won't come around in the future."

"In a different way."

"Perhaps." Maureen patted Emily's hand consolingly, then rose. "In the meantime, I promise to help you in any way that I can. We'll put the full power of the Fairfax name behind you and Bobby. And when that is done, this unfortunate situation with Brian's family quietly resolved, you and Edmund will once again be able to resume your normal lives."

Emily sensed a warning there. "Meaning what?" she asked, deciding impulsively to be as forthright and open as her new mother-in-law had been. "That you'll help us, but that you also want our marriage annulled, once the trouble with the Bancrofts is past?" If this was the case, Emily wanted to know now, before the situation between her and Maureen's son became more complex.

Maureen paused. It was clear she did not want to hurt Emily. Nor did she seem to want to be anything less than one hundred percent honest. "My son has been shortchanged once by Lindsey's untimely death. I know the two of you think you're in the same boat, and therefore have a tremendous amount in common. And I know the two of you have become friends, just as he and your husband Brian were. But, the bottom line is, I don't want my son shortchanged by a loveless marriage, no matter how compatible the two of you think you are."

COMPATIBLE OR NOT, Edmund sought out Emily and Chloe in the upstairs playroom only a few minutes later.

"I just had a fax from your teacher in Seattle," Edmund said, handing over the paper for his daughter to see. "She wanted to know how your assignments are coming."

Chloe ducked her head and concentrated on the handheld video game she was playing. "You know I haven't gotten any of them done yet, Daddy."

"Exactly my point, pumpkin." Edmund hunkered down in front of her so he and his daughter were on eye level with each other. "Don't you think you should get cracking on that schoolwork? With Bobby taking a nap, and Emily available to help you, and me working on farm business downstairs in the study, it'd be a great time to get a few assignments done."

"I'd like to, Daddy, really," Chloe said precociously, giving her father a winning smile, before going determinedly back to her game. "But school's been canceled today in Kentucky, on account of snow."

Emily grinned and gave Edmund a look, curious as

to what he was going to do. This was a real test for a parent. "She's got you there," she said mildly.

"Hey," Edmund teased as he angled a thumb at his chest. "You're supposed to be helping me here."

"Sorry," Emily replied in the same lighthearted manner, before turning her attention to Chloe. "Your Dad's right, kiddo," she said gently. "You probably do need to get caught up on your schoolwork. Maybe we could tackle one of the assignments right now."

"Any subject," Edmund added, willing to give his daughter as much leeway as possible. "It doesn't matter."

Chloe rolled her eyes in exasperation and put down her game. "Okay," she grumbled.

Unfortunately, as Emily soon found out, getting Chloe to concentrate was easier said than done. Though outwardly amiable, Chloe spent more time staring outside at the snow still lightly falling, than on her math. "Okay, one more problem," Emily said, after they had struggled through the other nine on the page of her textbook. "Then we'll quit for now and take a break."

"Hurrah!" Chloe said.

While Chloe skipped off to the kitchen to get a midmorning snack of milk and graham crackers, Emily wrote a short note, introducing herself to Chloe's teacher, and explaining she would be assisting Chloe in her lessons. She took that and the completed math lesson down to the study. Once there, she faxed both pages to Seattle.

"How's it going?" Edmund asked, as soon as he got off the phone.

Emily brought him up to speed, finishing, "She

gets the material easily, so it's not a problem of comprehension or understanding.''

"More like motivation.''

"From what I can gather, yes.'' Emily paused. "Has it always been this way? Has Chloe always disliked her schoolwork this much?''

His expression contrite, Edmund sat back in the chair behind his desk. "She used to love it. But after Lindsey died—well, it's been hard for her.''

Emily perched comfortably on the edge of his desk and folded her arms in front of her. "In what way?''

Edmund shrugged. "Lindsey used to spend a lot of time at the school as a volunteer. She was very involved in every aspect of Chloe's education. I think Chloe still misses having her there.''

"You could volunteer,'' Emily suggested. As a teacher, she knew there was always room for parent involvement. Charming, sensitive, gently teasing Edmund would be an asset to any classroom.

"I have volunteered.'' Edmund sighed and put down his pen. "As Chloe says, it's not the same.'' His eyes held hers. Remorse colored his low tone. "She wants a mother, Emily. It's as simple as that.''

Hence, he married me, Emily thought.

Edmund stopped, looked away, shook his head. "Maybe now that she's found one—'' he murmured.

Without warning, Chloe skipped into the study, part of a milk mustache on her upper lip. "Are you two talking about me?'' she asked, going around the desk to lean on Edmund's chair.

Emily nodded and smiled. This was Chloe's problem, too. It would take her help to solve it. "I was wondering what activity you liked best at your school in Seattle.''

"Show-and-tell." Chloe's eyes sparkled and her hands grew animated as she talked. "The kids always did funny things, and brought in neat stuff. It was the funnest part of the day."

As he watched his daughter, Edmund's eyes lit up, too. He looked intrigued. "You had it every day?"

Chloe nodded. "For a couple of minutes, yessirree, we sure did."

Well, Emily thought, it was a start. "You know," Emily told her new daughter with utmost casualness. "I know you're not in school here, but we could still have show-and-tell here, family style."

Chloe's eyes sparkled with excitement and she hopped up and down. "We could?"

Emily nodded. "If you want, we could also play a game I used to play with my third graders and have some bonus prizes for every assignment you complete. For instance, if you complete a language arts assignment today we could go out and have an—" Emily reached for the first prize that came to mind "— extra recess in the snow. Or we could play a board game together. Or whatever you want. We'll have to make up a list of suitable prizes we can both agree on, and then choose from those."

"Sounds fun to me," Edmund enthused.

Chloe scuffed the toe of her shoe on the rug and rolled her eyes. "Oh, Dad." A wealth of pent-up exasperation was in that one heartfelt sigh.

Edmund grinned, knowing, as did Emily, they'd at least caught Chloe's attention with this. "Is that a yes or a no?" he teased.

Chloe made an I-don't-know-about-this face as she surveyed the two of them for several long, thoughtful seconds. And in that instant, Emily realized here was a little girl who'd been made to grow up awfully fast the past year. It was understandable she'd rebel against the changes in her life somewhere. That somewhere was in her academic performance.

"You two're just trying to get me to do my schoolwork, aren't you?" Chloe surmised.

"Yes. We are," Emily said, making no bones about her teacherlike wiles. "And your dad and I will absolutely do whatever it takes to get you interested in your schoolwork again."

"So, what I want to know is—" Edmund paused. "Is it working?"

Chloe looked out at the beckoning snow, then looked back at her dad. She rolled her eyes in exasperation once more, slid onto his lap, threw her arms around his neck, and burst into giggles. "It sure is."

Chapter Six

"Look, Daddy, it's finally stopped snowing," Chloe announced the moment they stepped outdoors.

"It sure has," Edmund replied.

As Emily had hoped, the promise of a reward for her diligent efforts was all the incentive Chloe needed. As soon as lunch was over, she rolled up her sleeves and got right to work. Her language arts assignment finished, she went to tell Gail and her father. Both were delighted of course. In need of a break from work themselves, they swiftly decided to go outside with Emily, Chloe and Bobby to play in the snow.

"And look at this, everybody!" Chloe continued excitedly. "I'm walking on top of the snow!" Chloe did a pirouette, demonstrating. "I'm not sinking down hardly at all."

"It is pretty densely packed," Edmund noted as he knelt down to sift his gloved fingertips across the top of the foot-high blanket of snow that had turned the farm into a winter wonderland.

"It's the perfect consistency for sledding," Emily noted as she jostled a snowsuit-clad Bobby in her arms.

"And don't forget snow angels!" Chloe plopped down in the snow without warning and lay back, her arms flung out on either side of her. Sweeping her arms and legs across the snow, she swiftly made an imprint of an angel, wings and all.

"Down!" Bobby demanded, as he squirmed in Emily's arms and struggled to get down to where Chloe was. "Down!"

Emily set her son down carefully in front of her, so he was standing on the snow. Eager to explore on his own, he was still wriggling about, trying to be free of her. Nevertheless, she made sure he had his balance before she let go of his hands. As soon as she did, he promptly sat down on his bottom, fell backward in the snow, and began trying to copy Chloe's actions. Chloe giggled at her new brother's antics. Bobby joined in. Soon they were all chuckling.

"Talk about a snow baby!" Edmund chuckled. "This little guy was made for the winter weather!"

"He really does love it, doesn't he?" Emily murmured happily.

"Uh-oh," Chloe said as Bobby scooped up a handful of freshly fallen snow and smeared it across his face, getting as much as he could into his mouth.

Chloe sat up, helped Bobby to do the same, and then gently brushed the snow from his pink cheeks in an oddly protective gesture for such a little girl. "You're not supposed to eat that, silly," she chided softly. "You're supposed to pack it hard, into a ball, like this." Chloe demonstrated. "Then throw it at someone, like this." She aimed her snowball at her dad and tossed. It splatted on Edmund's coat, and disintegrated into a hundred tiny flakes.

Watching, Bobby grinned and gurgled back something unintelligible. Edmund laughed, too. "Better be careful or you're going to find yourself in a full-fledged snowball fight," he teased.

Chloe made an impish face at her dad, as if she couldn't wait. "Okay, but just so you know, you won't win," she teased right back.

"Hah!" Edmund retorted, a mischievous look in his eyes.

"I've got the sleds!" Edmund's sister Gail yelled victoriously as she strode toward them, bringing with her a saucerlike hard plastic dish with handles on the sides that was perfect for going down hills, and a sit-down, high-sided, wooden sled for toddlers.

"Can I pull Bobby around for a little bit?" Chloe asked, picking up the rope handle on the infant sled, as soon as Emily had Bobby settled in the seat.

"Sure," Emily said.

"Just be very careful," Edmund added.

"You two supervise while I take some pictures," Gail directed, taking out a pocket camera.

During the next few minutes, Gail snapped photos of Bobby in the sit-down sled, waving madly, while Chloe pulled him along, then photos of Chloe zooming down a gentle hill in her saucer sled while a gurgling, giggling Bobby cheered her on. There were more photos of Edmund, Emily and the kids, then Edmund took over the camera to snap a few shots of Gail with Emily and the kids, and finally Emily took over the camera to take photos of Gail and Edmund and the kids.

At last, satisfied they had pictures of everyone, Edmund and Emily stood back to watch Gail show Chloe the best way to roll balls of snow for a snowman. "Your sister is really great with children," Emily murmured.

"I know." Edmund nodded. "She's really taken with Bobby, too."

"He's really connected with her," Emily said, pleased.

"Too bad I can't say the same thing about you and my mother," Edmund said quietly.

Emily flushed, silently chastising him for having had the temerity to bring that up. "I don't know what you mean." She started toward the kids.

"Then let me spell it out for you." He caught her forearm in his gloved fingers and reeled her back to his side. "You two barely said two words to each other during lunch."

"So?"

Edmund gave her a deadpan look and edged nearer. "So I know when I've missed something," he stated in a low, gruff voice.

Emily took a deep breath and moved away from him just as determinedly. "You want to know what was said between the two of us?" Emily asked as her heart took on a slow, heavy beat. Damn, but she was in an awkward situation here.

The concern he felt for her was evident as he reached over to catch her in his arms and pull her close. "How'd you guess?"

Emily held his gaze with difficulty. "She offered to help us fight the Bancrofts."

Edmund smiled. "I knew she'd come around."

"Not that far around," Emily warned, her cheeks filling with heat. "She thinks we'd be better off friends than man and wife."

"We can be both," he assured her easily.

Could they? Emily wondered. "She also thinks, in allowing you to come to my rescue and marry me, that I've ruined any hope for you to have a decent romantic future."

Edmund looked at Emily meaningfully, letting her know with a glance they had not made a mistake, despite his mother's assertion to the contrary. "The day I let my mother run my love life—"

"She's got a point," Emily insisted stubbornly, averting her eyes from the tempting proximity of his sensually chiseled lips. "What if you do fall in love again?"

Edmund shook his head. "I won't."

He seemed so sure. "But if you do and I'm in the way of that—?" Emily's voice caught; suddenly, she couldn't go on.

Edmund laid his finger across her lips. "Didn't anyone ever tell you not to borrow trouble?" he asked softly.

Emily's chin set. "I can't help it. I feel guilty."

Guilty for robbing him of a future and entangling him in her problems. Guilty for breaking her promise to him already. She'd forced him to agree to keep this relationship of theirs platonic, yet already, after just one kiss and a mere eighteen hours of marriage, she couldn't stop thinking about the possibility of kissing him again.

What would happen tonight when that secret wish was flamed further by the sensual intimacy of them sharing a bed?

Edmund rocked forward. He grasped her gently by the shoulders and looked down into her face. "Don't," he scolded.

"But—"

"I'm a grown man," he said firmly, lacing an undeniably possessive arm about her waist. "I know what I want, Emily. And what I want is to be married to you."

THIS IS THE BARN where we keep our stallions," Edmund began as the five of them trooped into the first building in the horse complex. Constructed of concrete block walls and a metal roof, it was roomy, warm and immaculately clean. Tubs of grain were mounted to the walls of each stall. An automatic water basin provided fresh water.

"How many horses do you have here?" Emily asked Edmund as Gail took the kids over to see the two stallions in residence, Yankee Pride and Stormy Weather.

Edmund showed Emily around proudly. "Currently, we've got two stallions and the thirty mares the farm owns, plus forty colts and fillies being raised here."

Emily paused in the wide, cement-floored alleyway behind the stalls. "It looks like there are stalls for three stallions."

"We're down one right now," Edmund explained, frowning. "One of our studs was retired and put out to pasture last year. Mother has not been able to replace him on her own. Because of that, revenues were down sharply and we had to close three of the barns entirely."

"But this other horse you're after—King's Ransom—might change all that," Emily mused.

"Yes. If we get the owner's permission to put him out to stud here, then there'll be no shortage of people wanting to breed and board their mares and foals here.''

"Or in other words," Gail joined in the conversation as she returned with the kids, "it'd mean an immediate thirty percent upturn in business."

"That's a lot," Emily said, impressed.

"Yes, it is." Gail grinned at her older brother as she cuddled Bobby in her arms. "Which is why we're all counting on Edmund here to pull it off for us." She looked at Edmund. "Chloe wants Bobby to see the foals. Is it okay if I take them down to the yearling barn while you give Emily the four-star tour?"

Edmund quickly gave permission. Gail looked at Emily.

"It's fine with me, too," Emily said. "Thanks, Gail."

Gail and the kids took off, Bobby chattering every bit as actively as his new big sister Chloe.

Acutely aware of being alone with Edmund, Emily asked, "Can just anyone decide to have their horse bred here? Or do they have to own a racehorse, too?"

Edmund took Emily to the next barn where fifteen of the mares were housed in individual stalls. "Theoretically, anyone could. But the price of having a mare bred here would make it prohibitive to anyone but the most serious racehorse owner. Plus, we owe it to ourselves to be as selective as possible about the mares we want bred to our stallions, as the quality of the horses being bred on the farm have a great bearing upon profit. But typically, each stallion stands ten Fairfax Farm mares, plus twenty to thirty outside mares, depending on bookings."

Emily was impressed. "You have a veterinarian on staff here?"

Edmund nodded as he escorted her back outside. "And there's no shortage of work for him, since we have upwards of 120 horses here at any one time, now, year-round, and that'll increase to around 180 if we add a third stallion." They walked through the snow, around the premises, past several of the barns that were standing empty, Edmund telling her all sorts of interesting tidbits as they went.

"You seem to know a lot about the business," Emily remarked.

"I was supposed to take it over from my father when I graduated from college."

"But you didn't."

"No. I wanted to work as an investment counselor. Do something different. Live on the West Coast."

Emily both admired and understood his independence, yet she knew his decision had to have cost him. "Knowing your mother, she must've been unhappy about that."

Edmund nodded. "As was my father. For a while there, I was sure he'd never forgive me for walking away from all this." Edmund gestured around them. "But—" Edmund sighed "—he eventually respected my decision—my need—to become my own man, and build my own life."

"It must discourage you to see the downturn in business."

Edmund nodded grimly, admitting with a glance this was something that was weighing heavily on his heart. "I would've come home sooner had I realized how bad things were here in a business sense, but I didn't know," he said in a deep voice tinged with sorrow and regret. "My mother didn't give me the specifics when she called. She just said things were bad and she needed me here. His expression turned all the more penitent. "To tell you the truth, I thought she was exaggerating, until I saw the books."

"Maybe business will pick up on its own," Emily said hopefully. "Maybe this was just a low point in the cycle."

Edmund walked her through an indoor arena where grooms were currently exercising a few of the horses indoors. "I'd like to believe that," he said gruffly, as he led her over to the next building, the breeding shed, and walked her through the state-of-the-art facility and adjacent lab. "But I can't. I'm a numbers-on-the-page, facts-and-figures kind of guy. My dad taught me to take my emotions out of it, when it comes to making decisions. He believed that hard work and common sense would get me what I needed. He was always saying, *'Forget what you felt, forget about second-guessing others. What are the facts of a situation, plain and simple?'*" Edmund led her back outside, to view the various corrals and pastures behind the barns.

Emily paused in the crisp winter air. She leaned against the pasture fence and turned her face up to his. "Has his advice stood you in good stead?" she asked curiously.

His mood both thoughtful and self-deprecating, Edmund shrugged and answered, "In business, yes. In my personal life, it's been a definite detriment."

"I find that hard to believe," Emily murmured. In his roles as a husband and father he seemed so perfect to her.

"Believe it," Edmund retorted gruffly, shaking his head. He took her gloved hand in his and looked down at it. Absently, he stroked his fingers across her knuckles. "If I hadn't spent so much time shutting off my emotions, I might've—" He stopped, swallowed and didn't go on.

It didn't take a psychoanalyst to see the regret on his face was genuine and heartfelt. "What?" Emily asked curiously.

Edmund dropped her hand and turned away. The expression in his eyes was bleak and brooding. "I might've realized Lindsey was afraid. I might've stopped her from going out that afternoon, and in doing that, prevented her death."

Emily regarded him in shock. "Wait a minute, Edmund. Everyone knows that was an accident. Lindsey dashed out to get something from the grocery while you stayed home with Chloe, and her car spun out of control on a rain-slick street."

"Right."

"There was absolutely nothing you could've done to prevent that," Emily insisted firmly. "Nothing anyone could've done." These kinds of things just happened—there was no rhyme or reason to any of it.

"I know that's what everyone thinks," Edmund said softly. "But it's not true. I should've known that she'd always hated driving in the rain, that she'd always been afraid of losing control of the car in inclement weather. But I didn't," he said, his lips compressing grimly. "Hell, if one of her close friends hadn't mentioned it to me at the funeral, I wouldn't know even now."

Emily touched his arm gently. "I think you're being too hard on yourself."

He didn't seem to hear her as he stared at the low layer of opaque white clouds obscuring the horizon.

His voice was as tense and unforgiving as the set of his shoulders. "She was my wife, the mother of my child. I loved her and lived with her for eight years. I should have known she felt that way. I should have seen her phobia and sensed her feelings, even if she didn't come right out and say it."

"Maybe she didn't want you to know," Emily replied gently, desperate to offer whatever comfort she could. She stroked her gloved fingers down his forearms, to his wrist. "Maybe she was embarrassed by her fear. Maybe it was something she was struggling to overcome."

Edmund lifted a skeptical brow.

"Look, I know I barely knew her—"

"That's right," Edmund interrupted stoically. "You didn't know her."

Emily plunged on. "But in the brief time I spent talking with her at my wedding to Brian, Lindsey seemed like an exceedingly self-confident woman, a woman with a lot of pride in her ability to handle whatever came her way. She didn't seem like a woman who would admit to fear of anything."

Edmund paused. His shoulders relaxed slightly. "That's true. She was very capable."

"So maybe she wanted to protect you, in the same way that I wanted to protect Brian those first few weeks he taught in the juvenile detention school," Emily guessed.

Edmund pivoted to face her.

Knowing on this particular subject she had her own demons to wrestle, she began to pace back and forth, her boots crunching on the densely packed snow. "Once the kids got to know him and vice versa, and I realized how much the students he taught liked and respected Brian, I ignored the more pragmatic part of me sounding the alarm, and convinced myself there was nothing to worry about, that he would be okay there, because he was Brian, because the students adored him. But in the beginning, it wasn't so easy for me, 'cause I did worry. Then—'' Emily sighed and went back to stand next to Edmund again ''—I'd feel guilty about worrying, because I knew he needed me not to worry. So I made a point of not worrying.'' Emily swallowed hard around the knot of emotion in her throat. ''Then, when he was killed, breaking up a knife fight between two students he didn't even know, I felt bad,'' she whispered hoarsely. ''Because I knew—'' Emily splayed both hands across his chest ''—if I had just gone with my initial feelings and argued with him and prevented him from taking that particular job that he'd still be alive.''

Edmund sympathized, and more, understood. He reached out and touched her face. ''I know his parents felt that way—blamed you.''

''Yes,'' Emily said, for a second allowing herself the luxury of sinking into his touch. ''For a time, they did. But eventually, I realized, as did they, that whatever you call it—fate, God's will, karma—we're all on a path and stuff happens despite our best efforts and in the end we all live the life we're meant to live.''

''So no more regrets,'' Edmund ventured softly as he wrapped an arm about her shoulders and tugged her against his side.

''No. When we met and fell in love and married, Brian lived the life he wanted. He died doing work that meant the world to him.'' The tightness in Emily's throat eased as she once again found peace. Slipping her arm around Edmund's waist, she looked up at him and finished serenely, "I can't help but feel that wherever Brian is—'' Emily personally felt heaven "—he's still doing that. And so is Lindsey."

Edmund grinned. "You're probably right." He paused and looked down at Emily with affection, understanding, intimacy. Finally, he grinned again and stepped back, rolled his eyes. "We got awfully maudlin there, for a sec," he quipped self-deprecatingly.

"I agree." Emily was not one to sit around feeling sorry for herself, either. "It is definitely time to lighten up."

"Good idea." Edmund picked up some snow and cradled it playfully in his hands.

Emily flushed and backed up. "Don't you dare!"

"Too late." A snowball went whizzing by her collar.

"Too late for you, you mean." Emily scooped up two handfuls of snow and promptly got him back.

Within seconds of the hit, he caught her in his arms and pulled her against him playfully. "You're asking for it, you know," he teased. And suddenly, it seemed he was not talking about the snow she'd thrown.

Emily caught her breath as he angled his head over hers. That quickly, she knew he was going to kiss her again. What surprised her was that she wanted him to kiss her again, so much she could barely stand it. A thrill went through her. His lips lowered. She knew they shouldn't do this, but she no longer cared as their lips fused and she felt the need pouring through him. It had been so long since she'd felt this alive, so long since she'd felt so much hope. She threaded her hands through his hair, tipped her head up, stood on tiptoe so he could more thoroughly claim her as his. She let him kiss her until they both moaned and melted in each others arms; it was a stamp of possession that she felt all the way to her toes.

Realizing it was either stop now, or go back to the house and end up in bed, the two of them drew apart. "Edmund, I—" Emily fell mute at the unbearable tenderness in his eyes. She turned away from him, still aching and confused and so full of yearning she thought she'd die from it.

"I know." Edmund released a ragged breath and turned her face to his. "That really wasn't in the bargain, but it happened. So—"

"So we'll deal with it," Emily finished brusquely. They would have to.

He studied her, his expression impassive. "You're not upset with me?"

"No." How could she be?

"Good." Edmund sighed his relief. "Because I have something I want to ask you."

Emily's heart skipped a beat at the seriousness of his tone. Edmund rushed on. "If I wanted to stay here permanently, would you mind?"

Emily blinked, the abrupt change in subject throwing her off her guard. "What about your business in Seattle?"

Edmund shrugged, as if the transition were nothing he couldn't handle, financially or otherwise. "Some of my clients would leave, of course. Others would be happy to consult with me via phone and fax, and occasional trips to Seattle. Meantime, I could be closer to my family and keep an eye on the farm business at close range, while still doing the work I love, counseling investors." He paused, studying her upturned face. "I'd have the best of both worlds. Would that be okay with you and Bobby?"

Emily smiled. "I think this is a great place to bring up a family." *And fall in love.*

Edmund kissed the back of her hand. "I do, too."

One of the grooms stepped out of an office across the way. "Edmund! Phone for you! It's Mr. Thurston!"

"I better get it." Edmund released Emily reluctantly. "I've been playing telephone tag with him all day."

"Trouble?" Emily asked, when he rejoined her several minutes later.

Edmund scowled. "The Thurstons canceled again for lunch tomorrow."

Emily knew Edmund had been counting on a chance to recoup the couple's business. "Did they say why?" she asked sympathetically.

"They said weather, but that's not it."

"Then...?"

"They're afraid to face me."

"I'm sorry."

"So am I." Edmund was unable to mask his disappointment. "I'd really hoped they'd give me a chance to change their minds about going with a competitor."

That was easier said than done, Emily thought, if their longtime customers had lost faith in the business. "Maybe there's another way to get the business going," Emily suggested optimistically. "Some sort of new marketing approach. Different advertising. A more service-oriented approach, custom-tailored to each client."

Edmund looked glad she'd brought that up. "Actually, I have a few ideas I've been kicking around that would do just that—''

Before he could delineate said ideas further, the groom stepped out of the office across the way again. ''Edmund!'' he shouted. ''You're wanted up at the main house! Your mother has some news to tell you!''

Edmund waved in acknowledgment and thanks, then turned back to Emily. ''I hope it's good news.''

Emily tucked her arm through his. ''There's only one way to find out.''

EDMUND AND EMILY found Gail and the kids in the yearling barn, and headed up to the mansion together. Maureen met them at the front door. Selena was right behind her. Excited color highlighted Maureen's cheeks as she ushered them inside. ''It's official, Edmund. The owners of King's Ransom will be here to tour Fairfax Farm tomorrow.''

''How many other farms are in the running?'' Edmund helped Gail and Chloe take off their coats, then reached for Bobby so Emily could take off hers.

''We've got three other competitors,'' Maureen said. ''And I want Fairfax Farm to win Mr. and Mrs. King's business.''

They all did, Emily thought, as she slipped off her coat and snow-covered boots, too.

''I'll gather up the farm staff and apprise them of what's going on,'' Edmund promised, abruptly all business.

''I'll handle everything up here at the house.''

''I'll assist you, Maureen,'' Selena volunteered.

Emily noted Bobby was nearly asleep on Edmund's shoulder, and Chloe was looking pretty tired, too. The outdoor play and tour of the horse complex had done them all in. She reached for Bobby. "I'll take the children upstairs," she said, as Edmund gently transferred her sleepy baby to her arms.

· Minutes later, Emily had Bobby in a dry diaper and settled down in his crib, fast asleep. Chloe, who'd outgrown naps a few years before, but was still too worn out to attempt any more school assignments, had an agenda of her own. "Do you know how to sew stuffed animals?" Chloe asked, bringing in a threadbare Tigger who'd clearly seen better days. "'Cause my Tigger has a ripped ear."

"He sure does," Emily murmured, examining the black-orange-and-yellow toy. It took a lot of love to get a stuffed toy to such a fragile state.

Chloe seated herself cross-legged on her bed. "I'd take him to Daddy, but Daddy doesn't know how to sew."

"I'd be honored to patch up Tigger." Emily smiled graciously as she went to get her travel sewing kit out of her suitcase. Returning, she seated herself on the bed next to Chloe. "Although it looks as if it won't be the first time this little fella's had major surgery." Emily pointed to several neatly stitched places.

Chloe rubbed them with her fingers. "Mommy had to stitch him up a lot when I was little."

The loneliness in Chloe's voice made Emily's heart ache. "You miss your mom, don't you?"

"All the time." Chloe released a heartfelt sigh and propped her chin on her hand. "Does Bobby miss his daddy?"

"Bobby never knew his daddy—he died before Bobby was born."

The corners of Chloe's mouth turned down. "That's really sad."

"Yes," Emily commiserated gently as she threaded the needle, tied a knot, and snipped off the end of the thread, "it is."

"I was gonna have a baby brother once," Chloe confided.

Emily stopped sewing long enough to look up. "You were?"

Chloe nodded. "Before the accident," she explained, leaning over to get a closer look at her half-mended Tigger. "Mommy and Daddy said I was gonna have a baby brother, only I didn't get one, on account of Mommy died. That made me really sad. Daddy, too."

"It's hard, losing someone you love."

Chloe nodded, indicating this was so for her, too. She scooted to the end of the bed. "Want to see a picture of my mommy?"

Emily nodded. "Sure."

"Wait here. I'll go get one." Chloe went to her backpack and returned seconds later with a small picture that Edmund had obviously given her to carry around with her. It had been taken in Seattle, on a beautiful sunny day. Looking at the photo, Emily was reminded how much Edmund had adored his wife.

Emily was glad Edmund had married Lindsey. They'd loved each other and their marriage had produced Chloe, one of the sweetest little girls ever. But Emily felt an irrational pang of jealousy nonetheless. She didn't want Edmund to only like or desire her. She wanted more. The question was, did he want more, too?

"Hey! What are you still doing up?" Gail asked Edmund around midnight that evening.

Trying my best to save this farm, Edmund thought, as he tossed down his pen. "I thought I'd go over the proposed contract one more time."

Gail poured them both a nightcap. "Is King's Ransom the only thing on your mind?"

Edmund sipped his cognac and sat back in his chair. "What do you mean?"

Gail sat down opposite him. "I was referring to Emily's situation with the Bancrofts. I thought you might be up because you were worried about the possibility of a custody fight with them over Bobby."

Edmund pushed back his chair and moved to the hearth. There was no denying that Bobby had quickly become a son to him. "Do you think I should be worried?" he asked.

"In a word?" Gail watched him stoke the fire in the hearth. "Yes."

Edmund added another log, then replaced the screen. "Because you think it'll happen or because you think if it comes to that we'll lose?"

"Both."

Edmund dusted off his hands, stood. "Emily's an excellent mother." *And she'd make an excellent wife.* Not the platonic, best-friends-only kind they'd agreed upon when they'd entered this marriage. But the kind who'd share every aspect of his life and his bed.

Gail sipped her cognac. "No disputing that, brother dear."

"Then what are you saying?" Edmund demanded, unable to curtail his impatience.

"Simply this. Her hasty marriage to you leaves her vulnerable."

Which was, Edmund thought, the last thing he had wanted. "Vulnerable how?"

Gail spread her hands. "The court might view your actions as impulsive and therefore detrimental to both your children."

And they'd be right about the impulsive part, Edmund thought. He'd never acted so recklessly in his life. Nevertheless, his union to Emily still felt right, never more so than when he'd been holding her in his arms and kissing her again. "How would you suggest we counter that?" he asked seriously.

Gail smiled, glad he'd asked. "You and Emily could start by proving to people how much you and she truly are committed to each other—and to making this marriage of yours work."

"We are committed to this," Edmund said firmly.

Gail stood, drained her glass, and regarded him with a skeptical look. "Then why are you down here, brooding and alone, on what is ostensibly your honeymoon when your new bride is upstairs waiting for you?"

Good question, Edmund thought. He knew the answer, of course. His reluctance stemmed from the fact he shared the anxiety Emily did about sleeping together. He was afraid lying next to her in the dark, knowing they were man and wife in every sense but one, knowing she desired him as much as he desired her, would arouse him. He was disciplined enough not to kiss her again, no matter how much he wanted her, of course. What he couldn't do was stop from wishing she were already his in every sense.

But that was neither here nor there, he thought pragmatically as he said good-night to his sister, cleaned up the study, and switched off the lights. He did have to go to bed. And the time for that was now, Edmund thought as he headed up the stairs.

He looked in on Chloe and Bobby—both of whom were sound asleep—before heading to his own bedroom. He'd hoped to find it bathed in darkness. Instead, a soft light was glowing. Emily was propped up in bed, a book spread open in front of her, the baby monitor on the table next to her. Her glossy dark hair had been plaited in a loose braid that fell over her shoulder, her face scrubbed until it glowed. The gold-rimmed pair of reading glasses that slid down the bridge of her nose, made her look oddly studious and collegiate. Whereas the clothes she was wearing—soft pink flannel pajamas, emblazoned with giant snowflakes—made her look all soft, feminine and cuddly, and several years younger than he knew her to be.

Don't think about what's under those pajamas or how good she smells. Edmund loosened the knot of his tie. "What are you reading?"

She held up the spine of the book, so he could see. Edmund read the title aloud. *"Breeding Horses for Idiots."*

"Your mother gave it to me. She wants me to bone up on the subject before Mr. and Mrs. King arrive tomorrow."

Probably a smart move, Edmund thought. In no hurry to undress, Edmund sat on the edge of the bed. "How's it going so far?"

Emily shrugged and laid the book across her chest. "Actually, it's really interesting." She peered at him over the top of her glasses. "How is your part of the preparations going?"

Edmund tore his glance from the graceful U of her

collarbone, and the silky texture of her skin. Looking back at the spine of the book, he caught the shadowy cleft between her breasts, visible in the open V of her pajama top. He felt perspiration dot his brow. Blood rushed to the precise place he did not want it to go. "I've got the contracts about ready. I still want to go over them one more time, but they are as beneficial to the Kings as we can make them, without losing money on the deal, so I'm confident we've got a strong bid."

"Good."

An awkward silence fell between them, broken only by the soft sounds of their breathing.

She slid the glasses a little farther up the bridge of her nose. "Are you coming to bed now?" she asked softly, curiously. "Or are you just in here to change clothes?"

Edmund made an offhand gesture. He gritted his teeth, girded his thighs, and did his best to contain his desire. "I thought I would unless you want to read some more."

"No." Emily clutched her book more firmly to her chest. "I'll be ready to turn out the light whenever you are."

Chapter Seven

What a dumb thing to say, Emily thought, as Edmund disappeared into the adjoining bath, nightwear in hand. *I'll be ready to turn out the light whenever you are.* Could she behave any more awkwardly or ill at ease? It wasn't his fault they had to share a bed this evening. Nor, in the course of the days, weeks and even years ahead of them as man and wife, was it likely to be an isolated occurrence.

So she might as well get used to it now.

Which was, she thought, easier said than done as he came out of the bath, clad only in soft gray sweatpants that cloaked his masculinity like a glove, and a white V-necked T-shirt that did equally impressive things for his broad shoulders and muscled chest.

He slid into bed, smelling of toothpaste and cologne.

Emily put her book aside, took off her glasses and turned off the light. Unfortunately, no sooner had she settled back, albeit somewhat stiffly on her side of the bed, and he settled back on his, than they heard it— a faint drowsy whimpering, coming from the baby monitor.

She started to rise. Edmund put a hand out to stop her. "I'll get it."

He vaulted from the bed, swept soundlessly across the plushly carpeted bedroom and padded out into the hall. On the other end of the monitor, Emily heard only silence. Two minutes later, Edmund returned. "Must have been dreaming. He's still fast asleep."

Emily shifted slightly to face him. "Sorry you had to get up."

"No problem. I enjoyed looking in on him."

You want to know. So ask. "Edmund?"

"Hm?"

Okay. Here goes. Emily bent her arm at the elbow and propped her head on her upturned palm. "Chloe said something this afternoon," Emily told him quietly, "about you and Lindsey having a baby before she died—"

"Lindsey wasn't pregnant, but she wanted to be." Sadness crept into his low tone. "We both wanted a son."

Emily's heart went out to him; she knew how it felt to have your dreams dashed in an instant. "And Chloe knew that?"

"We thought it best to prepare her for the possibility, before it actually happened, rather than just spring it on her after the fact. What about you?" Edmund stroked patterns with his fingers on the stretch of covers between them. "Did you and Brian want other children?"

"Oh, yes." Emily watched the mesmerizing stroke of his fingertips. "Three or four, as a matter of fact," she said softly.

And now, thanks to the miracle of her hasty marriage, she suddenly had two children and so did Edmund.

"Do you still want more children?" He covered her hand with his.

"I don't know." Emily's fingers quickly absorbed the sexy heat of his. "Prior to coming here—" Emily rolled onto her back and stared at the ceiling "—I'd completely given up on the possibility. But being here—marrying you—taking Chloe into my heart so quickly, I realized there are other ways to expand my family."

"Such as adopting," he guessed, as if he, too, had considered just that.

"Artificial insemination, and so on," Emily concluded. *And let's not forget the old-fashioned way, of just making love with your husband.* Where had that thought come from? Emily wondered shocked. It wasn't as if she and Edmund had a real marriage.

Edmund shifted onto his back, too.

"So, how was your evening?" he asked, letting go of her hand.

Lonely, Emily thought, *without you.* Aware he was still waiting for an answer, she said, "Quiet. Gail was busy going over the contracts with you. And your mother and Selena were totally caught up in planning the menus for the Kings' visit tomorrow."

Edmund frowned, perturbed. "Selena's really trying to muscle in around here, isn't she?"

So he'd noticed, too, Emily realized with equal parts satisfaction and pique. "If you don't mind my asking—exactly what kind of past do the two of you have anyway?"

"I've known her since we were kids. She used to come visit her aunt and uncle every summer."

"So you were friends," Emily guessed trying—and failing—to picture the easygoing, chivalrous-to-the-core Edmund paired with the high-strung socialite.

Edmund made a comical face that let Emily know just how far off the mark she was about that. "Not exactly. There was too much of an age and interest differential for that, but I escorted her to cotillion a couple of times as a favor to her aunt and my mother."

"Who were matchmaking even then," Emily presumed.

Edmund nodded. "I knew she had a crush on me. I figured it would fade when I didn't ask her out again. Instead, it just got stronger. My marriage to Lindsey and move to Seattle took me out of her sights for a while. She even got engaged to another guy. But when that ended a couple of months ago, she set her sights on me again," he finished unhappily.

"With her aunt's and Maureen's help."

Edmund nodded. "I think they all had this fantasy I'd see her again, realize what a mistake I made in overlooking her the first time. And our two families would be joined via holy matrimony forever." He released a beleaguered sigh.

"Instead," Emily continued with a rueful grin, as she inhaled the clean, wintry scent that was uniquely his. "I show up—"

"Even before Selena, as it happened," Edmund interjected.

"And win your hand in marriage."

"Right." Edmund paused. For a second he was moodily silent. "She'll get discouraged again and set her sights on someone else, I know it."

Emily wasn't so sure about that. Selena did not

seem as though she were going to go down without one heck of a fight.

Edmund touched her arm. "Look. If you want me to talk to her—to ask her to quit edging you out on household stuff or chores with my mother—"

"No." Emily put up a silencing hand. As much as she loathed Selena's ongoing interest in Edmund, a request like that wasn't going to be fair. "I'm so busy with the kids," Emily said. "I know your mother needs the help. It's fine with me if Selena assists." There was absolutely no reason for her to feel the tiniest bit jealous and she knew it.

Edmund searched her face. "You're sure?" he asked.

Emily nodded. "Positive."

Edmund sighed and fell into a brooding silence as he turned his glance out the window. "I just hope the Kings don't change their mind about visiting and are able to get here."

Emily frowned and shifted toward him once again. "What do you mean?"

Edmund rolled to face her, too. "I checked the weather before I came up to bed. The blizzard isn't over yet. Another slow-moving snowstorm is on the way, and it may hit us as early as noon tomorrow or as late as tomorrow evening."

"Is this storm supposed to bring a lot of snow?" Emily asked, doing her best to ignore the sexy warmth of him.

"Maybe another six or seven inches. Which means, of course, it'll be that much longer before we can get the pipes fixed in the cottage."

Emily groaned. The aroused way she was feeling, the sooner they stopped sharing a bedroom and a bed, the better. "They weren't kidding when they described this as The Snowstorm of the Century."

"We'll be out of the main house eventually," he teased.

"I'll hold on to that thought," Emily teased right back.

"In the meantime, we better get some shut-eye. The kids are going to be up awfully early."

Edmund looked at her as if sleep were the last thing on his mind, but—ever the gentleman—he kept to his side of the bed. His gaze roved her from head to toe, generating heat wherever it touched. "That being the case... How do you sleep?" he asked casually. "On your back or on your side?"

How about in your arms? "Usually on my side," Emily replied, irritated to find her voice sounded a little hoarse and breathy. "You?"

"On my back."

They shifted around, her hip bumping his side, his knee hitting her thigh. Finally, they were set. "Comfortable?" he asked softly.

As I'll ever be with you this close to me, Emily thought. "Yes." Emily closed her eyes against the romantic aura of the moonlight streaming in through the windows, but could do nothing about the sexy scent that was uniquely him. She swallowed around the sudden dryness of her throat, asked huskily, "You?"

"Mmm-hmm." He reached over, took her hand and brought it to his lips for a nice, platonic kiss. "Good night, Emily."

Emily breathed a sigh of relief he had not tried to take undue advantage of their close quarters. "Good night," she said, as he dropped his hold on her, settled comfortably on his side of the bed and clasped his hands behind his head. It wasn't disappointment she felt, that he hadn't really kissed her, she thought as he closed his eyes and prepared to go to sleep. It wasn't, it wasn't, it wasn't...

AN HOUR LATER, a cold shower was beginning to sound really good. Maybe because Edmund had not anticipated just how difficult it would be to be that close to Emily and not touch her. At least not deliberately. Keeping a sleeping Emily from touching him was another matter entirely.

Exhausted no doubt from all the activity of the past few days plus caring for a baby, she had clutched a pillow to her chest, curled up on her side, and gone to sleep within five minutes of turning the light out. Five minutes after that, she'd planted one dainty sock-clad foot squarely against his calf. He wouldn't have thought that would be erotic; it was, almost unbearably so. Before he could do anything to slow his abruptly erratic breaths, his heartbeat had taken on a slow, thudding beat, and his lower half had gone into overdrive.

Attempting to allay his growing desire for her, he turned onto his side. Thinking maybe if he faced away from her, he wouldn't be inhaling the sweet, sexy scent of her hair and skin, or be drawn to the fragile warmth of her. To little result. No matter how tightly he closed his eyes, he couldn't forget the enticing slope of her breasts or the gentle curves of her hips beneath her flannel pajamas. Nor could he stop the surge of desire and protectiveness he felt whenever he was near Emily.

He had never expected to love another woman, but

he could easily fall in love with Emily for reasons that went beyond the purely physical. Beyond loneliness. Or the need for a loving mother for his child. He could fall in love with Emily for reasons that came straight from the heart.

The question was, did she feel the same?

If not, would she?

To Edmund's chagrin, Emily slept as restlessly as he did. Nevertheless, she was at his side later that morning when he got the initial report from the private investigator over the telephone.

"There's nothing in the Bancrofts' past to imply they'd be anything but exceedingly generous guardians to their grandson. In fact, it's a certainty they'd fulfill their promise to put him in the very best private schools, take him on twice-yearly trips to Europe and see he had every luxury imaginable."

No way out there, Edmund thought, disappointed. "What about during the past year—since their son died?" Edmund demanded. "Anything out of the ordinary there?"

"No. They've been living the high life with a vengeance, as per usual. Taken several trips abroad. Entertained lavishly."

"What about business?" Edmund asked, holding his coffee cup to his lips. There had to be a clue here somewhere.

"Whit Bancroft doesn't actually work at anything, you understand. Just dabbles in this and that. I did hear he's considering becoming a founding partner in a business that'll sell discounted computers over the Internet, but that's it on that score."

Edmund drank deeply of the steaming coffee. "Is their marriage in good shape?"

"Yes, though they've apparently made no secret of their frustration with Emily—they want her to go live with them in the mansion and she won't. They're betting a judge will find her continued refusal to accept their generosity equally incomprehensible. Hence, the custody suit, which they are certain they will win."

Not if I can help it. "What's their next move?" he asked crisply.

"Just what you'd think," the detective confirmed. "To force Emily to either relinquish Bobby to their care, or in to family court. Her leaving the state—and marrying you—has slowed them down. But not necessarily deterred them."

Which meant, Edmund thought, he and Emily still had a lot to do.

Edmund hung up the phone and filled her in.

Emily slowly put down her own coffee cup. A distant look in her eyes, she stood and began to pace the study. "I suppose on the surface it does look strange that I won't go live in their mansion, but I know if I were to give in on that, it'd be no time at all before they were hounding me on the rest." She moved to the window and stood looking out at the snow. Her glossy black hair caught the light reflected from the snow and tumbled to her shoulders in thick, sexy waves. "Brian didn't want our child jetting all over the world before the age of three and going to pricey private schools. He wanted him playing sandlot ball, attending public school, working a part-time job, all the things his parents denied him. He felt he'd grown up in a glass bubble, that he'd missed out on an awful lot of everyday all-American life." Emily paused and turned to face him. Embarrassed color pinkened her cheeks. "I don't mean to sound critical. I know you went to boarding school, too."

"Only high school," Edmund amended, strolling nearer. He fastened his gaze on the deep sea blue of her eyes. "As a kid I went to the local elementary school and junior high in Sweet Briar through eighth grade. And believe me, that period of my life was about as far from Brian's jet-setting childhood as you can get. I mucked out the stables and groomed horses on a regular basis, did Scouting and league sports, and spent a fair amount of time standing in line at the local Dairy Queen."

Emily's full, luscious lips curved into a self-effacing grin. "Sounds like my childhood, with the exception of mucking out the stables. I did a lot of household chores, instead."

"You had a happy childhood?" Edmund asked.

"Yes. You?"

"Very."

Silence. Emily shook her head and shoved both hands through her hair. "Who'd ever think that in itself could be such a detriment in the end?"

Edmund edged closer, drinking in the clean, sexy fragrance of her perfume. "What do you mean?"

Emily sat on the edge of his desk. Her sigh was part wistfulness, part frustration. "Sometimes I think I might have been better off if I'd had a little more adversity in my youth, if things hadn't always gone the way I wanted them to go." Planting her hands on either side of him, she tilted her face up to his. "Instead, I was a protected and much adored only child who glided smoothly through my adolescence and college years. Whatever I wanted, I got. However I felt things should be, they were. When I did see signs something probably wasn't going to work out the way I wanted it to, I ignored them, and kept right on going. I had this feeling that if I wanted something badly enough I could make it happen, through a combination of hard work, committment and desire. And Brian felt exactly the same way. He had the same kind of invincibility I did. Unfortunately—'' Emily sighed again ''—that doesn't excuse my own stubbornness. Even after all that's happened, even after losing first my parents and then Brian, I can't seem to face the way things are instead of the way I want them to be or feel they ought to be. Because if I could do that, Edmund, I would have seen this custody-suit move on the part of the Bancrofts coming. I would've known they weren't going to back off. I would've known that even more trouble lay ahead.''

"WHAT DO YOU THINK, Emily? The wide bands or the thin?'' the jeweler asked several hours later.

"I actually like the thin unisex bands the best,'' Emily told the jeweler who had come out to Fairfax Farm to meet with them. She studied the velvet display case of wedding rings in front of them, then glanced up at Edmund, anxious for his opinion. "What about you?''

"I like the idea of us having identical bands.''

"Two-tone or solid platinum or solid gold?'' the jeweler asked.

"Solid gold,'' Emily and Edmund said in unison.

"Would you like to have diamond insets, either channel or baguette?''

"I think I'd prefer the plain,'' Emily said.

"Same here,'' Edmund agreed.

"Swiss cut, fluted or antique?''

"I like the bands with the fancy, sort of braided edges," Emily said.

"That's the Swiss cut," the jeweler said, as he sized Emily's finger.

"I like it, too—in gold," Edmund agreed.

The jeweler searched out the appropriate band in his case. "Try this on your wife, for size," he told Edmund.

Edmund took Emily's left hand in his. He slid the delicate gold wedding band on her finger. The ring did what the ceremony, the vows, even sleeping in the same bed hadn't. It brought a feeling of reality and permanency to their relationship that was not to be denied.

"How does it feel?" Edmund asked.

Like I'm really married. Like soon we'll both be saying to heck with common sense or prior agreements and sharing a lot more than a bed.

Aware he was waiting for her reply, and that it should be something suitable for the jeweler to hear, she said softly, "It's a perfect fit." *As could be my life here.*

Without warning, Selena barged in carrying two vases of lavishly arranged flowers. "Oh, dear, am I interrupting something?" she asked impishly.

Knowing, Emily thought, full well that she was.

Her back to Emily, Selena set a crystal vase down close to Edmund. "Your mother wanted these brought in from the greenhouse right away." Selena paused significantly as she continued to ignore both Emily and the jeweler; and instead, fastened her bright-eyed gaze on Edmund's face. "She and I are personally arranging the flowers in honor of Mr. and Mrs. King's visit."

Edmund nodded appreciatively at the painstaking arrangements of white roses. "They're lovely."

Selena's glance dropped to the velvet-lined jewelry case. Her lips formed a skeptical moue. "Rings?"

"It's time we got around to it, don't you think?"

Selena lifted her slender shoulders in a shrug. "I suppose given the fact the Kings are coming it would be wise for you and Emily to be wearing them," she agreed, her eyes lifting to Edmund's. "Appearances, you know."

Or, in other words, Emily thought resentfully, the rings were—in Selena's opinion anyway—every bit the stage prop the flowers were. Meant to set the scene for a history-making deal and nothing more.

The jeweler, clearly fearing he was about to lose a sale, inserted himself between Emily and Edmund. "Emily, perhaps you'd like to assist Edmund in trying this on," the jeweler said.

And show off in front of Selena? Emily quickly realized she'd like nothing better. A warm flush of color filling her cheeks, she took the ring from the jeweler. Aware of Selena's resentment-filled eyes upon her, Emily took Edmund's hand in hers. It felt just as she knew it would—warm, strong and faintly callused. Nevertheless, her hands trembled as she slid the ring on his finger, and it was all she could do to push it past his knuckle.

Edmund regarded it. "Just like yours. A perfect fit," he said.

Selena regarded Edmund like an experienced golf pro regarded a challenging shot. "If you'll excuse me." She nodded politely at everyone, then deliberately focused on Edmund, murmuring, in an oddly intimate tone, dripping with sensuality, "I'll see you later." She turned on her heel and left the room.

If Edmund caught the promise in her low tone, he did not seem aware of it. But there was no way Emily could avoid it. The vows Emily and Edmund had taken meant nothing to Selena. She still wanted Edmund for herself. She seemed determined to win his affections. Emily wondered uncomfortably just how far Selena would go to get Edmund to notice or become more intimately involved with her.

Minutes later, Edmund had paid for two identical, Swiss-cut gold bands. The jeweler—worried about the advent of yet another snowstorm that had paralyzed most of the northeastern half of the nation—was on his way.

Edmund pocketed the receipt and returned to Emily's side. "I should pay for half the price of the rings," she said. *And I should also forget Selena. She's no threat to me. I have nothing to be jealous of there.*

Edmund shook his head. "It's on me."

"I better check on Gail and the children."

He caught her arm and pulled her back to his side. The sparkle in his eyes had her immediately on her toes. "These rings make it official, you know," he teased.

"I know."

"It won't be long before everyone gets the message."

Without warning, Emily couldn't seem to get her breath. "And what message would that be?" she asked coquettishly.

He threaded his hand through her hair and tilted her head beneath his, to precisely the right angle.

"What message do you think?" he asked her as he brushed his lips ever so gently across hers.

Oh my. Emily stared up into the handsome contours of his face. "Edmund, I—" she murmured helplessly, melting against him.

"That's it," he whispered, as his lips touched hers, evocatively at first, then with gentle pressure. "Say my name, Emily," he murmured hoarsely. "And I'll say yours. Over and over and over again—"

A thrill swept Emily from head to toe. She trembled in his arms as her knees went treacherously weak. "Edmund." *Edmund.* His lips molded to hers. He kissed her long and thoroughly in a way that made her want much, much more. With a low moan of surrender, Emily pressed against him, aligning the warmth of her body to the warmth of his. Caught up in the intensity of what she was feeling, Emily was only dimly aware of the sound of the doorbell in the distance. Footsteps on marble. Much more acute was the sensation of his lips moving on hers, his body against hers, and the fact that whenever he held her like this that she felt alive again—wholly, wonderfully, truly alive.

So what if none of this was going to be simple or easy, she thought, as he swept a hand down her spine, urging her closer, so her breasts were crushed by the hardness of his chest, the depth of his need for her and hers for him no longer any secret.

The two of them could make this marriage of theirs work, she decided determinedly. And they could love each other, too. All they had to do was want it badly enough. All they had to do was love each other in this deeply fundamental, deeply tender way.

And it was then, when she was ready to give her

all to him, that she heard the horrified gasp behind them.

"Emily," two familiar voices thundered. "Just what in heaven's name do you think you're doing?"

Chapter Eight

Edmund had never liked Brian Bancroft's parents. Seeing the way the blond, elegantly slim jet-setters looked at Emily, as if she were some piece of street trash, made him like them even less.

"I think that'd be obvious," Emily replied in answer to Andrea and Whit Bancroft's question as Mrs. Hamilton ushered in their guests, and then quietly shut the doors behind them. "I'm kissing my husband."

"We're not idiots. We witnessed that much," Andrea Bancroft replied haughtily as she looked askance at Emily's casual outfit of denim blue stirrup pants and a matching high-necked, tunic sweater emblazoned with Disney characters. Then turned with equal distaste to the Fairfax Farm flannel shirt and cords Edmund wore.

"We were referring to your hasty marriage to this scoundrel who called himself Brian's friend," Whit said stiffly.

"Have you taken leave of your senses?" Andrea demanded, looking as elegant and cultured as ever in a red Chanel suit and Gucci boots. "Getting married so swiftly?"

"Come to them, is more like it," Emily murmured back, with the same daunting lack of politeness.

"It's not too late to get an annulment, with the right lawyer," Whit advised.

"I don't want an annulment," Emily retorted defiantly.

Nor do I, Edmund thought. "It's nothing to be ashamed of, dear," Whit continued. "Everyone will understand you've been under tremendous strain."

Emily sighed and turned her head into Edmund's shoulder. "Never more so than right now," she whispered in his ear.

Edmund kept his snug grip about her waist and pressed his lips to her ear. "Want me to take over?"

She stood on tiptoe and murmured, so only he could hear. "Would you?"

"Gladly." He kissed her earlobe, then turned to their guests.

"I think the real mystery is how you two were able to get here so swiftly," Edmund said.

"It wasn't easy," Whit said, pulling out his pipe.

"We had to deice our jet repeatedly while waiting for clearance to take off, fly into a private airstrip southwest of here, and hitch a ride on two snowplows."

"But we managed," Andrea said, taking a seat on the edge of the sofa, "because this is important."

Whit nodded as he sat beside his wife. "We love our grandson, Emily, and we don't want to see him brought up as anything but a Bancroft."

Emily took a seat on the sofa opposite them, as did Edmund. "Bobby will always be Brian's son. I'll make sure he always knows his father."

Andrea shook her head. "It's more complicated than that."

"Obviously," Edmund agreed, "since you were planning to sue Emily for custody of Bobby."

Shock filtered across Whit and Andrea's faces. They looked at each other, then back at Emily and Edmund. "How did you—?"

"Does it matter?" Edmund asked abruptly, not about to give them the details on whom, when, where and how Emily had been tipped off about their actions.

"It's true, isn't it?" Emily added wearily as she put her hand in Edmund's and held on tight.

"We've made no secret of the fact we want you and Bobby to come and live with us," Andrea said stiffly.

Emily placed her hand on her heart. "And I've made no secret of the fact I don't want to do that."

"You can't go back to teaching, Emily," Andrea said cooly.

"That," Edmund interjected, tightening his hand over hers protectively, "is for Emily to decide. Although as my wife, she is certainly free to be a stay-at-home mom, too."

Emily shot him a grateful look.

"Is that why you married him, Emily?" Whit asked, too cordially. "For his money and the carefree life-style he can provide?"

Edmund stared the Bancrofts down. "Emily is not on the witness stand."

"Though I am quite capable of speaking for myself," Emily added, looking as if she'd about had it trying to defend herself and her actions to her in-laws.

"Good," Andrea immediately responded, "because I'm quite intrigued by what you have to say about the reasons for this elopement, Emily dear.''

Unfortunately, Edmund thought, the truth would not come off very well. As Emily looked at him, he could tell she was thinking the exact same thing. Loathe to lie. Even more reluctant to tell the truth. Silence stretched between them.

''Well?'' Whit prompted impatiently. ''We're waiting.''

''I think the larger question,'' Edmund replied, ''is why you felt it necessary to come here in person.''

''To dissuade you from making a temporary mistake a permanent one,'' Andrea explained.

''But if it's not going to happen—'' Whit continued, tamping tobacco into his pipe.

''It's not,'' Emily said.

''Then we want to help in any way we can,'' Andrea continued pragmatically.

''And we understand if you want to start your life all over again,'' Whit said, pausing to light his pipe.

''What you don't need, Edmund,'' Andrea continued smoothly, ''is another man's child interfering with your relationship with Emily. And certainly not when you've just begun your marriage to her.''

''I see,'' Edmund retorted, knowing a well-orchestrated plan when he saw one. ''And you're offering to do what exactly?''

Andrea flashed a winning smile. ''Take full custody of Bobby. If not permanently, then just for a few months.''

''WHAT ARE THEY UP TO?'' Edmund asked Emily short minutes later as they dressed for the formal business luncheon with the Kings.

Aware they hadn't much time if they both wanted to be ready to greet the potential clients upon arrival, Emily sat on the edge of the bed and kicked off her soft suede ankle boots.

She looked up at Edmund.

You don't buy their 'Newlyweds need time alone, to get their marriage off on the right start spiel,' either then.''

"Not for a second." Edmund stripped off his flannel shirt and cords and went to the closet to get out a navy Brooks Brothers suit, starched pale blue shirt and tie.

Edmund frowned. "You know what gets me? I know Whit and Andrea neglected Brian terribly when he was a kid. Half the prep school holidays he had no one to go home to, so instead he went home on break with me and half a dozen other friends.''

Emily brushed against him as she reached for her sage green wool suit. Still tingling from the accidental contact, she stepped behind the screen. "I've never seen them do anything that didn't benefit them directly." They had been indulgent, selfish, self-centered and hedonistic.

"So why do they want Bobby so much?" Edmund wondered out loud as, still buttoning her suit jacket, Emily stepped out from behind the screen.

Emily shrugged. "It can't be for the million-dollar trust fund. They have tons of money and a very lavish life-style on their own." She picked up a brush and tugged it through her hair. "Until today, I thought it was because Bobby's their last link to Brian, and in Bobby, they saw a chance to make up for past mistakes and do it right this time.''

"But you no longer think that's the case," Edmund

theorized slowly, as he zipped up his trousers and slipped on his shirt.

"No. And you know why?" Deciding her hair needed to be up, Emily swept it up into a French twist, and secured it with copper-coated pins. "Because they're not emotional about this. They talked about custody of Bobby, but they weren't all that eager to see him."

Edmund joined her at the mirror, to knot his tie. "So what's their real agenda, then?" he asked, looking at her in the mirror.

Emily added blush to her cheeks and outlined her lips a becoming shade of rose. "I don't know." Emily turned to face Edmund as she clipped on her best pearl earrings. "I get the sense they're in a panic about the idea of me bringing up Bobby on my own."

"I get that sense, too, though why they'd worry on that score is beyond me. You're a great mom."

"Thanks."

Emily searched through her jewelry pouch for the necklace that went with her earrings. Finding it, she slipped it around her neck. "Maybe they're afraid, if left to my own devices that I'll squander all of the money Brian left for Bobby in trust, or bring Bobby up in a manner that is just too middle class."

Edmund stepped behind her to fasten the clasp. "Money is not what kids need." Finished, he placed his hands on her shoulders and turned her to face him. "It's love and attention and plenty of loving care, and you give Bobby all of those things in abundance."

"Just as you give them to Chloe," Emily said, glad they shared the same values. And because of that, and the fact Edmund was so bighearted, she knew Edmund would make Bobby an excellent father.

"But…?" Edmund prodded, when she didn't go on.

Emily swallowed around the knot of apprehension in her throat. "It's just we're not out of the woods here yet, with Whit and Andrea. They've said what they had to say and they still won't leave. Which can only mean they're here to try to find something to use against me in court."

Edmund shrugged. "So, let them take the full tour of the farm and look their fill. All they will discover is that this is a great place for you and Bobby to be."

Emily couldn't argue that. "What if it starts to snow again, before we can ferry them back to their jet?"

Edmund glanced at the clock, aware, as was Emily, that the Kings were due to arrive in less than fifteen minutes. "Then we'll be wonderful hosts and offer them shelter for the night."

At his continued nearness, Emily's heart took on a heavy beat. "And suppose they won't leave the day after that, either?"

Edmund grinned, not the least bit nonplussed about what to do. "Then we'll continue to offer them shelter until they're so sick of us they'll want to leave," he teased.

Emily lifted a lecturing finger. "You laugh this off now, but you don't know what you're letting yourself in for here. Whit and Andrea are extremely critical and demanding. I mean, you saw the way they looked at my Disney sweater."

"For no good reason, too," Edmund quipped, his glance roving her from head to toe. "You looked very cute in that sweater."

Emily blushed at the compliment, and the desire underlying it. "You're missing the point."

"No, I'm not. They're snobs," he declared.

"Huge snobs."

Edmund shrugged his broad shoulders and did not take his eyes from her face. "Then they've met their match, because when push comes to shove my mother and Selena can be every bit as snobby as they can."

Emily couldn't disagree with that, especially in Selena's case. She regarded Edmund, exasperated. "It could be a disaster here." She didn't want to see him or his family hurt.

"Not if we don't let it." Edmund wrapped his arms around her and massaged his way down her back. "Besides, you strike me as the kind of woman who can handle damn near anything. Which, by the way, is probably what has Andrea and Whit so worried. They know—deep down—they are not going to get the best of you no matter how many dirty tricks they pull."

Emily relaxed in the warm security of his arms. Maybe Edmund was right. Maybe she was overreacting here. The bottom line was the two of them wanted this to work. Hence, together, they'd find a way. "You're full of compliments today," she murmured. And his compliments made her feel great.

Edmund grinned, a playful light in his sable brown eyes. His eyelids lowered as he admitted huskily, "Yeah, well, you inspire them in me. And for the record, I meant what I said about your sweatshirt," he told her tenderly, as he curved a hand alongside her face. "You looked perfect in it."

"Thanks." Emily turned her head and impulsively kissed his palm. "For the record," she said, as she paused to straighten his tie, "you look pretty cute in Fairfax Farm flannel, too."

"It's the only thing to wear when doing a nitty-gritty inspection of the stables in this weather."

They joined hands. Together, they headed for the door. "I didn't have a chance to ask you before the jeweler got here. Is everything all set for the Kings' visit?"

"Yes." Edmund glanced at his watch again. "And they should be arriving any minute."

WHILE MRS. HAMILTON AND HER teenage niece took care of Bobby and Chloe during the afternoon, Emily stood as Edmund's wife to help host the Kings. Meanwhile, Selena, as a personal favor to Maureen, made sure the Bancrofts were otherwise amused during the long business-oriented afternoon. As expected, the formal luncheon, tour of the farm facilities and initial business meetings with the Kings went very well. But nothing could've prepared Emily for Maureen's request when she pulled Emily aside as the dinner hour approached.

"I want both children present this evening during dinner."

Emily hesitated. "I don't know if that's wise, Maureen. Chloe can handle it, certainly, but Bobby is awfully tired—"

"Nonsense! He and Chloe were both angels during the noon meal."

"I know they were." Mr. and Mrs. King, Whit and Andrea Bancroft, even Selena, had all been so impressed with the children's quiet demeanor. They couldn't have behaved more angelic if they'd tried.

She, Edmund and the children had looked like the perfect all-American family.

"Mr. and Mrs. King are very family-oriented people," Maureen continued sincerely. "They selected our farm, and two others, because our farms are run by family. One last show of family unity can only help us snare their business."

Emily knew how important it was to Edmund, to have King's Ransom turned out to stud on the Fairfax Farm. Edmund had gone the extra mile for her and Bobby. It was time she and Bobby went the extra mile for him. "What time would you like us in the dining room?" she asked cordially. Maybe, if she was very lucky, there was time for a short nap in between.

Maureen smiled, pleased. "Seven."

"We'll be there."

Unfortunately, Bobby—who'd slept only thirty minutes earlier in the day—was in no mood for a late nap, no matter how Emily rocked, sang or cajoled. As a contingency measure, she took a bottle of milk and a small bag of his favorite alphabet blocks with her for his high chair tray. Then made sure she and the children arrived just seconds before they were all to sit down.

To her relief, dinner started out tranquilly enough. Mr. and Mrs. King could not stop talking about the first-rate operation of the farm. They made it through the soup course, and the salad, but by the time they started the main course, Bobby'd had enough. He simultaneously pushed the spoon of mashed potatoes away from his mouth and made a grab for it. "Mine!" he announced.

Emily shook her head, letting him know by her disapproving expression that this was not going to fly with her tonight. Still holding his glance, she wiped the mashed potatoes from his fist, and offered him another spoonful.

This time Bobby grabbed the spoon with both hands and held on tight.

"Bobby—" Emily warned softly, aware all heck was about to break loose, just as she had feared.

"A child is never too young to learn table manners. Just tell him no—firmly," Whit Bancroft advised swiftly.

"I think Emily can handle it," Edmund interjected, fixing Whit with a no-nonsense gaze. "And if not, I'm here to help."

"Mine!" Bobby shouted unhappily, as he attempted to wrestle the spoon away from Emily.

Flushing as all eyes turned to her and Bobby, Emily tried once more to pry the sticky spoon from his grasp, and was rewarded with a piercing yell from her misbehaving son.

Emily didn't care what anyone else said or thought. As far as she was concerned that was it. She wiped her hands on her napkin, pushed back her chair, and stood. "This young man is saying good-night," she announced pleasantly to one and all. "Say good-night to our guests, Bobby."

"No!" Bobby yelled, then burst into sobs of fury, as he lunged forward and tried—once again without success—to recapture the mashed-potatoes-covered baby spoon.

Calmly, Emily slid back the tray of his chair, and reached over to undo his belt. Still screeching indignantly, Bobby grasped on to the sides of the high chair and held on tight. Her face nearly as flushed and red-hot as her son's, Emily grasped him beneath the arms and tried to pick him up into her arms. Bobby responded by going suddenly, completely limp. Emily would've had a hard time managing his twenty-five pounds of weight even in the sturdiest, flat-soled shoes. In delicate high heel, it was ridiculous. She felt herself tottering backward, even as Bobby continued to screech. In unison, six chairs screeched backward, as everyone attempted to come to her and Bobby's rescue at once.

But it was Edmund who caught her, and took Bobby out of her arms. With a grin that said these kinds of calamities just happened with kids, he drawled, "We'll be right back, folks."

"I am so sorry," Emily whispered, rushing after them, as Edmund carried the still-screaming Bobby from the dining room. And he was still hollering when they reached the nursery.

"I think this is what they mean when they say a child is overtired," Edmund deadpanned.

"And then some," Emily said, holding out a bottle. She didn't know when she had been so embarrassed.

Gail appeared in the doorway. "Everything all right up here?"

"It'll be fine," Emily said, getting out pajamas. "As soon as I get him to sleep."

Gail grinned. "Lotsa luck." She turned to her brother. "Are you coming back down?"

"Not for a while. Just continue without us."

"Maybe you should—" Emily said, as Bobby kicked and flailed and screamed his little heart out.

"And leave you to deal with this little rascal alone?" Edmund teased.

As if there were no place in the world he would rather be, Edmund picked Bobby up and put him against his shoulder. While Emily watched, Edmund paced back and forth, rubbing Bobby's back gently and talking all the while. "You've had a heck of a day, haven't you? Here you are, dead tired, wanting only a story and a bottle of milk and maybe a nice turn or two in the rocking chair with your mama— who, because she's been so busy helping me today, has had very little time for you—and then these silly, silly people make you sit through a boring business dinner, what could they be thinking? I know, I know. They weren't thinking, were they?"

On and on Edmund talked, gently and soothingly. Eventually, Bobby's sobs turned to hiccups, then quieted altogether. He curled his body into Edmund's chest and rested his head on Edmund's shoulder. He pressed his face in the curve between Edmund's neck and shoulder and curled both his little arms around Edmund's neck.

Seconds later, his eyes were closed. His breathing was deep and even, tempered only by the occassional hiccup. He was asleep.

Chapter Nine

Together, Edmund and Emily put Bobby ever so gently into his crib, tucked his teddy in with him and covered him with a blanket. Simultaneously, both breathed a sigh of relief and turned to face each other. "Oh, Edmund," Emily whispered. "Your jacket—" The shoulder of his suit coat was smeared with mucus and tears. "You can't go back to the dinner table looking like that."

Edmund glanced down. He made a face. "I see what you mean," he countered grimly.

Lifting his eyes back to hers, he grinned and tucked a finger beneath her chin. "Although I'm not the only one worse for wear. You've got mashed potatoes in your hair." He held out a strand. Sure enough, tiny white flecks were stuck to the long black hair.

Emily released an exasperated breath. "I guess he did us both in."

"And then some."

Emily took Edmund's hand. "Come with me. I'll have you fixed up in no time." She paused to switch on the baby monitor, then led Edmund into the adjoining bathroom. She patted the counter with a delicate hand. "Sit here."

Content to let her call the shots for a moment, Edmund sat on the counter, legs spread. Damn, but she looked pretty, he thought, even after a long and trying day. "Do you want me to take my jacket off?"

"Actually," Emily said, her soft lips pursing together thoughtfully as she studied the stain, "I think it'd be easier if you left it on, if you don't mind."

"No problem," Edmund retorted easily, realizing a bit too late it wasn't that great an idea to have her standing between his spread legs. But there was no getting out of it as Emily dampened a washcloth with warm water and wrung it out. Flattening one hand between his shoulder and the inside lining of his suit jacket, she pulled the fabric taut, and being careful not to get the fabric too wet, gently dabbed at the stain. Her gaze fastened solely on his jacket, she said in a low distracted voice, "Thank you for putting him to sleep."

Edmund studied her easygoing manner and generous smile and wondered what it would be like if she fell for him, too. "My pleasure," he said softly. "Besides, that's what dads are for."

Emily tossed him a rueful look. "I don't think all dads are as good at handling cranky babies as you are."

Edmund basked in the compliment. "I aim to please."

Unable to make as much progress as she liked, she stepped closer and rubbed a little harder.

"I'm sorry Bobby kicked up such a ruckus."

Edmund struggled to ignore the intimate feeling of her hip, rubbing up against his inner thigh. "It wasn't his fault. He should never have been at that dinner this evening."

"I won't argue with you on that." As Emily blotted his jacket with a towel, her breasts brushed lightly against his biceps. "I should have known better than to let myself get pressured into bringing him." Her delectably kissable lower lip curled into a frown of utter dismay. "Believe me, it's not a mistake I'll make again," she confided softly. "When he's too tired, he's too tired."

Edmund smiled and concentrated on the satiny slope of her neck. "I'm sure Bobby will be glad to hear that."

Emily paused. She surveyed his appearance carefully. "There." Both hands on his shoulders, she turned him to the mirror. "How's that?"

"Great. However—" Edmund grinned at her mashed-potatoes-flecked hair "—you, still need some work."

Emily started and looked at the mirror. "I can't believe I almost forgot about that."

Edmund stood, put his hands on her waist, and helped her sit on the counter still warmed by his body heat. "Allow me."

Her legs shifted gracefully to the side of his, she sat stock-still while he worked the strands beneath his fingertips. She wished they could stay up here forever, vulnerable and alone. She wished she could touch him the way she wanted to touch him.

"There." He slid his fingers beneath her chin and tilted her face up to his. "I think that's it," he said softly, smiling at her with purely male satisfaction. "You're all done," he told her huskily. "Except for one more thing."

Emily's eyes widened. Her lips parted. "What's that?"

"This." Taking full advantage of her vulnerability, he covered her mouth with his own. His lips closed over hers, brimming with a hunger she hadn't known he possessed. Before she knew it, Emily was kissing him back, totally. He leaned back to look at her, then covered her mouth again in a searing kiss. Feeling she'd been waiting forever to find happiness again, to find passion and pleasure, she let him wrap a hand around her hips and guide her to her feet. Her knees felt weak as he pinned her between his body and the counter, but she stood on tiptoe anyway and arched against him. Had she ever felt this way before? she wondered as his tongue sizzled along hers, circled it and flicked across the edges of her teeth before dipping deep.

Had she ever wanted this desperately or completely? She only knew she wanted him to kiss her and touch her and yes—even love her!—until all the hurts in their pasts, until all the grief and the loneliness and the despair went away. Until just the beauty of the present and the tantalizing magic of their future was left....

Edmund hadn't meant to do any of this. He knew it was dangerous to start anything that might shift the balance of a relationship so new. But with her so near—and the lust and the love within him so strong—he found he could not walk away.

Before he knew it, one kiss had turned into many. Desire flowed through him in hot waves as she met the thrust and parry of his tongue with a kiss that was warm and sweetly tender. His lower half pulsing with desire, Edmund cupped the soft curve of her bottom and held her against him.

Knowing there were guests waiting downstairs for

both of them, Edmund drew back, a crazy mixture of emotions running riot inside him. As much as he wanted to make her his—now and forever—this moment was not the time. But the time would come. He was more certain of that than ever as they breathlessly drew apart.

"I WAS GOING TO ASK what took you so long," Gail teased, as Edmund and Emily rejoined the group. "But one look at the two of you and I think I know."

Emily had been afraid that would be the case, despite the fact she'd taken time to repair her lipstick and make sure her hair was in place before they'd returned to the others guests. Try as she might, she'd been unable to do anything about the sparkle in her eyes or the warm flush of excited color that came into her face whenever she was near him. To her satisfaction, Edmund looked just as pleased with the growing intimacy between them as she was.

"It's true. Both of you have that just-kissed-glow about you," Mrs. King remarked with a smile. "But then, what would you expect from newlyweds? I'm sure the last thing you two lovebirds want to be doing this evening is entertaining."

How true that was, Emily thought on a wistful sigh. She'd much rather be curled up in the cottage with Edmund, before a roaring fire, with the kids asleep in their beds, and the snow falling softly outside. But that wasn't going to happen as long as the plumbing problems there persisted. No, until the broken pipe was repaired and the water in the cottage turned back on again, they were stuck in the main house, with all eyes upon them.

"You know, the two of you should be alone," Mrs. King continued.

On that, it was clear, Selena Somerset did not agree.

Alerted by Mrs. Hamilton there was a phone call for him, Edmund excused himself. When he returned, he was once again all business. "I'm afraid I'm going to have to run out on you folks once again. We've got a mare about to deliver. And I want to be there."

"Any chance we could watch?" Mr. King asked hopefully.

"It'd give us a real feel for the place," Mrs. King said.

"Certainly you can watch," Maureen Fairfax said, already surging to her feet. "I'll come along, too. Gail?" Maureen looked at her daughter.

Gail smiled. "Count me in."

"What about me, Daddy?" Chloe asked.

Edmund frowned, his disinclination to give permission apparent. "It's awfully late, pumpkin."

"I don't mind. I can sleep late tomorrow. Please." Chloe clasped her hands in front of her in silent supplication. "It's been so long since I've seen a horse born and you know how I love it!"

"I'll be happy to go along and bring her back early if she tires out," Selena volunteered.

"Please, Daddy, please?" Chloe begged.

"Okay. You can go." Edmund cast a speculative look at the rest of them. Wary of being that far from Bobby, Emily passed on the invitation. In short order, the Bancrofts also declined. The others trooped out. Emily took her baby monitor and was about to head for the stairs. The Bancrofts cut her off at the pass.

"Emily, if you don't mind, Whit and I would like to speak to you alone,"

Emily wanted to refuse but she figured she might as well get it over with. Experience had taught her the Bancrofts would not back down. They retired to the study.

Andrea began, "This show you and Edmund are putting on is not fooling us a bit."

Emily sat down on the sofa, still cradling the baby monitor in her hand. "I don't know what you're talking about."

"Then we'll spell it out for you, dear. Fairfax Farm's in financial decline and has been since Edmund's father died a year ago. Maureen's unable to cope and the burden is on Edmund to solve the problem."

"None of that has anything to do with me," Emily said.

Andrea gave her a condescending smile. "That's where you're wrong, dear."

"Didn't you think it odd when Edmund began writing you after Brian died?"

Unable to sit still for their false innuendo a second longer, Emily surged to her feet. "He and Brian were close friends."

"Back in their prep school days, yes," Whit agreed, readily enough. "After that, they drifted apart to the point, in recent years, Brian and Edmund only saw each other at their weddings."

"That's because they lived on opposite coasts and were busy with their jobs."

Whit took out his pipe. "If Edmund was so close to Brian, why didn't he attend his funeral?"

Emily was holding on to her composure—and her

temper—by mere threads. "Because his own wife had just died and he didn't know about it until it was too late. So he wrote to me instead."

"And—?" Andrea's brows rose in mockingly polite inquiry.

"And it took me months to answer," Emily explained.

"And then what?" Andrea demanded.

"He wrote again," Emily replied, her voice rising right along with her agitation at being falsely ridiculed and accused. She began to pace. "Eventually, so did I. And over a period of time, the letters became more frequent."

"Yet you didn't mention any of this to us," Whit muttered disparagingly, his resentment about that fact obvious.

Emily lifted her hands helplessly. "You were in Europe at the time. And the letters were personal. They were about coping with single parenthood."

"He preyed on your vulnerability, Emily," Whit told her.

Emily shook her head, refusing to believe it. Edmund had not—would never—played her for a fool. "He was vulnerable, too."

Andrea inclined her head and exchanged rueful looks with her husband. "More so than you know."

Whit nodded. "We had a chat with Selena earlier. The Farm has been in trouble for months. Edmund and his mother both know they needed something like a big infusion of cash to jump-start it and get it going again."

So? Emily released an exasperated sigh. "I don't have that kind of money."

"But Bobby does," Andrea reminded.

"Don't you wonder why Edmund rushed you into this hasty marriage?" Whit asked, his smooth, cultured voice dropping an insinuating notch. "Don't you wonder why he gave you so little chance to think about it, or even less to change your mind?"

"Because he knew he was going to have to prey on your emotions and act fast to access Bobby's one-million-dollar trust fund."

Emily stared at Whit and Andrea, her blood running hot and cold simultaneously. "That's a lie," she said.

"Is it?" Whit challenged.

Andrea shrugged. "Someone's going to have to invest the money and keep tabs on it. He's a financial advisor—and from all accounts, a damn good one."

"Good enough to raid Bobby's fund without you knowing it was even happening," Whit agreed.

"You're wrong," Emily said hoarsely.

"Are we?" Whit replied. "You heard his alternate plan, Emily. If he doesn't win the contract to put King's Ransom out to stud here, then he's going to buy a host of top quality mares, breed them to top quality studs via artificial insemination, and then put them up for auction two years from now."

"At which time he should realize a hefty profit and get the farm back in the black."

"In the meantime, someone's going to have to pay for all that. Who's it going to be, Emily?" Andrea demanded. "Where is he going to get the initial outlay of cash for the additional broodmares and the cost of impregnating them? Where's he going to get the money for all the feed and staff and utilities and farm upkeep, not to mention advertising and so on? It won't be coming in from other owners, because he's going to be the one underwriting the costs for half the broodmares here.''

Whit smiled. ''We know where he thinks he's going to get it, of course—from Bobby's trust fund.''

''But he's wrong about that,'' Andrea smiled furiously, ''because we are not going to allow him to use Bancroft money to save a Fairfax business.''

''And once Edmund realizes that he'll drop you like a hot potato.''

''Edmund does not want Bobby's money,'' Emily said firmly. *He wants me—first in his life, then in his arms, perhaps next in his heart.* ''He married me for me,'' Emily continued.

''Emily, Emily.'' Whit and Andrea both shook their heads in silent remonstration. ''You have always been too naive, though we don't deny there are other reasons that factor into this as well. One, his daughter needs a mother—preferrably someone who's good with children. And two, he needs someone to run his household for him.''

''I don't deny that,'' Emily said, fighting for calm. ''But there's more to it than that.'' *Our growing feelings for each other. Our determination to make this union of ours work.*

''Right. He also wants a woman to warm his bed. But for the two of you to pretend to be falling in love right before our eyes—'' Whit Bancroft stopped and shook his head.

''It isn't happening, Emily,'' Andrea continued flatly.

''And it isn't going to happen,'' Whit continued grimly. ''As soon as Edmund realizes he isn't going to get control of Bobby's trust fund through you, he'll give up on this ruse and send you and Bobby on your way.''

Anxiety warred with rage. ''You're mistaken about this, about all of it,'' Emily said tersely, even as she felt her confidence in Edmund and her marriage wane.

Whit and Andrea gave her a pitying look. ''Time will tell,'' Andrea murmured. ''Won't it?''

Chapter Ten

Emily was curled up on the window seat of their bedroom, looking out at the softly falling snow, when Edmund returned. It was midnight but he looked as if he still had a ton of energy left as he kicked off his shoes, and stripped off his suit coat and tie.

Emily knew exactly how he felt. The kisses they had stolen in the bathroom earlier that evening had left her feeling revved up and ready to go. The seeds of doubt Whit and Andrea had planted in her mind had left her edgy and restless.

His brown eyes on her face, Edmund began unbuttoning his shirt, starting at the neck and working his way down. "I thought you'd be asleep by now," he remarked quietly as he crossed to her side.

Emily had been determined to regard him with an unbiased, unsentimental view, but it was a decision easier made than rendered when he was standing there in front of her, his sable hair windblown, a few stray snowflakes still glistening in his hair, his cheeks red from the cold. "I wanted to wait up for you," she said, forcing a smile. *I knew I wouldn't be able to sleep until we talked.* "So." She drew a bracing breath, stood and tried to still her racing heart. She put the book she'd been pretending to read back on the shelf. "How did it go down at the stables?"

Bypassing the usual gray sweatpants, Edmund grabbed a pair of expensive-looking silk pajama pants from the drawer and swiftly disappeared into the bathroom.

"Great. The foal's healthy as can be, despite coming a little early."

Emily listened to the downward rasp of his zipper, the jingle of his belt, the whoosh of a shirt being pulled off, and clothes hitting the hamper. Keeping her back to the half-closed door, she continued, "I presume Mr. and Mrs. King were pleased."

"Very. Though I don't know that they are any closer to signing a contract with us for King's Ransom." Edmund paused to brush his teeth.

Worried of their voices carrying, Emily stood and went to the bathroom door. "If they don't, and you go ahead with your alternate plan, how much is all that going to cost?" *Please tell me Whit and Andrea are wrong in their assertions, that you already have a source of capital planned out.*

Edmund finished rinsing his mouth and blotted his face with a towel. Turning, he tossed it on the countertop, and still appearing to be a little distracted, he ran a hand over his cheeks and chin. "I don't know." Frowning at the evening stubble of beard his fingertips encountered, he picked up his electric razor and switched it on. "I've been so busy working on other avenues I haven't sat down and run through the figures just yet."

A trickle of unease ran down her spine as Emily watched him run the razor across his face, obliterating the shadow of beard that had begun to appear.

Trying not to wonder why he was shaving so late at night when he could just as easily wait until morning, she continued to press him for more details on his alternate plans to save the farm. "Just a ballpark figure," she urged softly.

"Well, let's see." Edmund compressed his lips together thoughtfully as he ran the razor across upper lip, obliterating even the barest hint of dark mustache. A reflective light came into his dark brown eyes. "Thirty additional mares at an average price of twenty-five thousand each comes to around eight hundred and fifty thousand. Add in stud fees of ten thousand or so for each mare—that adds another three hundred thousand."

Which, Emily realized, feeling a little sick, put him over one million, without even adding in anything else like upkeep, staff, feed, medicines, and so on. Her heart sank. "With the farm doing so poorly, do you have that kind of money available to you?" she asked curiously.

"No." Edmund shook his head unhappily, then continued determinedly, "I'll have to find investors willing to go in with me."

Emily met his eyes in the mirror. Her gaze drifted lower, to the feathery sable brown hair that spread across his broad shoulders and superbly muscled chest, and disappeared into the waistband of his clinging silk pajama pants. "You couldn't mortgage the farm to raise the cash?" she asked, trying not to think what might have led Edmund to choose such uncommonly sexy attire for bed.

"No." His own thoughts seeming similarly—and oddly—distracted, Edmund splashed aftershave between his hands and slapped some on his cheeks, the underside of his jaw, his chin. "My father's will prevents us from ever using the farm or any of the equipment as collateral."

I see. Her arms folded beneath her breasts, Emily lounged in the portal. "And a bank wouldn't give you a business loan."

"Not without collateral." Edmund spun around to face her, his eyes squarely on her face. "Why do you ask?"

Oh, no reason, Emily thought.

He leaned against the sink, his legs spread slightly, his hands cupping the edge of the marble countertop on either side of him. He looked her up and down, taking in her flannel-covered body from head to toe. "What is it?" he asked gently. "What's wrong?"

Emily shook her head. "Nothing." She felt incredibly disloyal for even listening to Andrea and Whit for an instant.

"C'mon, Emily." Edmund drew her into his arms, situating her cozily between his spread thighs. "I know we haven't been married very long, but I know something's up," he said softly. "Now what's bothering you?" he asked as he carefully searched her face.

The touch of him against her, with only their flimsy nightclothes between them, was like molten lava running through her veins. Adding the memory of the scorching kisses they'd shared earlier in the evening was like adding gasoline to the already blazing inferno.

"Tell me," he insisted.

Emily knew she was in a no-win situation here. If she blurted out some baseless accusation, he might never forgive her. And if she didn't—if she let herself and Bobby be used because she was too proud to come right out and lay it all on the line and ask—she'd never forgive herself.

"Does it have something to do with Brian's parents?" Edmund asked. "Did Whit and Andrea Bancroft say something to you while I was out at the barns?"

She swallowed and shrugged, unable to tell him her doubts. "You know them. They, well, they've never approved of me."

A dangerous look came into Edmund's eyes. "So they did give you a hard time."

She flattened her hands across his bare chest. "They came here to do that. We both knew that from the get go."

Unable to bear any more of his questions, she vaulted from his lap and swept from the room. Edmund followed her into the bedroom, to the bed. She sat down on her side. He sat down on his. "What did they say, Emily?"

Emily unbelted her robe and kicked off her slippers. Swinging around to face him, she held up a silencing palm. "I don't want to get into it, Edmund. Not tonight." *Maybe not ever.*

His eyes darkened as she shrugged out of her robe, slipped beneath the covers, and turned off the light on her nightstand. "Damn it, Emily." Edmund released an exasperated breath. "I want to protect you."

She knew that, Emily thought as her heart began to race. Didn't she?

She lay back on her pillow. Edmund shifted over her. "You're right," he said softly. "Enough talk about the problems in our life." He drew her into his arms once again. "We've got better things to concentrate on," he said in a low, husky voice. "Like us." Just that swiftly, his head lowered. Her eyes shut. And then there was a muffled staticky sound, followed by a low, anguished wail, coming from the baby monitor beside the bed.

Emily and Edmund frowned in unison, as the crying became high-pitched and frantic. "It's Bobby—" Emily said.

"And it sounds like something's really wrong!"

As soon as Emily picked up Bobby, and saw him rubbing his lip and biting down on his finger, Edmund knew what the problem was, as did Emily. "Poor sweetie," Emily said, rubbing Bobby's back and walking him back and forth, attempting to soothe him. To no avail, he kept crying hysterically. "He's getting a new tooth."

"No wonder he was so cranky at supper," Edmund sympathized. His gum was so red and swollen it had to hurt like the dickens.

Looking almost as distressed and upset as her son, Emily inclined her head in the direction of the changing table. "I've got some medicine for it in the diaper bag."

Edmund plucked out the tube of numbing gel Bobby's pediatrician had recommended. The directions guaranteed it would work to stop the discomfort within sixty seconds of applying it, but it was clear it was going to take both of them to apply it, so Edmund held Bobby while Emily rubbed the cherry-flavored gel gently over his swollen gum. As soon as she had finished capping the tube, Bobby held out his arms to her. She took him back into her arms. Holding him close, she continued to walk him back and forth, talking to him soothingly all the while. To little avail. Bobby's cranky sobs continued unabated.

"What else can we do for him?" Edmund asked.

Emily looked down at her son, her heart going out to him. She bit her lip and kept her distance. "A bottle of milk would probably help him get back to sleep."

Edmund was relieved to be able to offer additional help. "Say no more. I'll go down to the kitchen to get it."

She smiled at him in a brisk, impersonal manner and turned her eyes away. "Thanks," she said quietly.

Was it his imagination, Edmund wondered as he pulled a baby bottle from the fridge and went to get a pan of water to warm it, or was Emily relieved to get him out of there and put some distance between them? He couldn't help but contrast her attitude now with her attitude earlier, just after they'd gotten Bobby to sleep, when they'd kissed. Had they not had both family and dinner guests waiting on them, he was certain they would have made the short journey from bathroom to bedroom, fallen into bed and made love.

Now, just hours later, she seemed wary and excessively polite in lieu of relaxed. Now, she looked at him as though the intimate conversations and passionate kisses they'd shared had never happened, as though she didn't know him at all. Edmund didn't know what was behind the change in attitude, but he didn't like it one bit.

"I thought I heard you come down here."

Jerked from his reverie, Edmund turned to see Selena standing in the doorway. She was wearing an ice blue satin-and-lace negligee that left very little to the imagination.

Had Emily been wearing such a garment, it would've taken his breath away, and prompted him to take her into his arms and then into bed for some lusty, uninhibited lovemaking.

But to see Selena in such a blatantly seductive garment left him feeling only embarrassed for both of them.

Deciding it best to pretend her gown was not nearly as diaphanous as it was in the bright kitchen light, Edmund turned away. "Couldn't sleep?" he asked, concentrating on the bottle warming in the pan.

"No," Selena murmured huskily as she drifted to his side in a cloud of exotic perfume. "Nor could you."

Pretty sure this was a come-on, Edmund kept his eyes averted and cleared his throat. "Actually—" he began.

"I know just how you feel," Selena interrupted huskily as she sashayed around him provocatively and planted herself between Edmund and the countertop in a manner that left Edmund feeling as though he'd landed in a Mae West movie.

Selena ran her bloodred fingertips through the mat of hair on his bare chest. "I couldn't sleep, either."

Recoiling from the unwanted advance, Edmund caught her hands in his and removed them from his skin as politely but firmly as possible. He supposed he was responsible for this. He'd known she had a crush on him and, rather than address it directly for fear of hurting her feelings and damaging the long-standing friendship between his family and hers, he had chosen to ignore it as opposed to tell her point-blank that he was not interested in her and never would be.

He looked at her, communicating all that and more in a single glance. "It's late," he said meaningfully. *Go away.*

To his chagrin, Selena either did not read his feelings accurately, or she chose to ignore them. "Don't I know that," she murmured seductively.

Edmund looked her straight in the eye. "I'm married," he said flatly. *Off-limits.*

Again, Selena stubbornly refused to get the hint. "Now, Edmund, you and I both know that's not true," she disagreed in a silky tone, as she swished over to the other side of the room, and turned off the overhead light, so that only the dim stove light remained. "Whatever it is you and Emily have going for you, it's not a real marriage."

But Edmund was willing to bet the farm his marriage would've been real by now, had the Bancrofts not said or done whatever they had to upset Emily while he was out at the barns and Bobby had not awakened, crying. Had either of those two events not happened, he reasoned as he turned away from Selena's annoying presence, he would be up in that bedroom, making love to Emily with all his heart and soul right now. And she'd be making love to him in the same heartfelt, passionate way.

His patience with his former date exhausted, Edmund reached for Bobby's still-warming bottle. "Do us both a favor, Selena," he said harshly, "and go to bed. Now."

He planned to do the same—with Emily—as soon as possible.

"Oh, I'll go to bed, all right," Selena said as he tested Bobby's milk on his wrist and found it to be exactly the right temperature. "But first I want you to turn around and look at me one last time," she said.

So much for her not humiliating the both of them further, Edmund thought. Determined to do whatever he had to do to get rid of her, Edmund turned.

Setting the bottle aside, he swore and snatched up the transparent gown she'd discarded. "Are you nuts?" He tried to cover her and drape it around her, but she shrugged him off, proudly delighted by her nakedness.

"We're in the kitchen, for heaven's sake!" Edmund fumed, part of him unable to believe this was really happening, especially tonight of all nights! "What if someone else comes down here?" he demanded, in a panic, aware the lessons in chivalry he'd received as a kid had never covered anything like this. "What if my mother or Whit and Andrea Bancroft or Mr. and Mrs. King come down here?" he demanded in an effort to scold some sense into her. "What would they think?"

But the situation was past saving. "I don't care," Selena pouted as she launched herself into his arms. "I'm tired of hiding my feelings, pretending to all the world we're just friends!" she said stubbornly. "I want everyone to know how I feel about you, Edmund!" she cried passionately, grabbing his biceps and thrusting her naked breasts against his bare chest. "I want everyone to see us together—"

"Congratulations," a cool voice said from the doorway. "You've gotten your wish. On my behalf, anyway."

Edmund pivoted in the direction of the voice. Damn it all to hell! *"Emily."*

Lower lip trembling, her face white as chalk, she said, "I came down to tell you to forget the bottle—I already rocked Bobby back to sleep. I can see I needn't have bothered," she finished primly, "as it wasn't high on your list of priorities anyway."

Edmund held out a beseeching hand. "Emily, give me a chance to explain—"

Her gaze averted, she dashed off.

Edmund swore. Selena grabbed his arm. "Let her go, Edmund."

"I don't care if you are an old friend of the family. I don't care if it's snowed another foot by then," he said savagely. "I want you out of here, first thing tomorrow morning."

Leaving Selena behind, he rushed after Emily. It was no surprise to find the door to their bedroom was shut. It was also locked.

EMILY HEARD EDMUND try the door once, twice, then a third time. Finally, he moved away. Tears rolling down her face, she unbelted her flannel robe and climbed into bed.

She didn't know what was going on. All she knew was she had never felt so upset and humiliated in her entire life. Was Edmund having an affair with Selena? About to? Is that why he had initially agreed so readily to a platonic arrangement with her after they married? So he could continue to sleep with Selena?

Abruptly, a key turned in the lock. A split second later, the door to the bedroom opened. Edmund came in, his whole body girded for battle. "It wasn't the way it looked, Emily,'' he told her as he strode masterfully for the bed, and sank down beside her.

Emily jerked away when he tried to grab her hands. She sprang from the bed. ''How dumb do you think I am?''

Edmund vaulted after her. ''Selena heard me come downstairs. She followed me and took off her gown.''

Emily paced back and forth, aware she had never wanted to slug a man as much as she wanted to slug Edmund at that moment. She whirled on him so suddenly she almost slammed into his chest. ''Just like that—with no encouragement from you?''

Edmund towered over her and regarded her stonily. ''Pretty much, yeah.''

Emily planted her fists on her hips and glared up at him. ''That is the lamest explanation I've ever heard!'' she fumed.

Edmund did not take his eyes from hers. ''But it's true,'' he countered firmly.

''True or not—'' Emily shrugged ''—it'll be a cold day in hell before I ever kiss you again.''

Edmund looked as if he had expected as much. ''And why is that?'' he asked, as her chest rose and fell with each furious breath.

Hot, embarrassed color flooded her cheeks as she tried without much success to get the image of what she had stumbled on in the kitchen from her mind. ''I don't like being played for a fool.''

Edmund continued to look at her as though he had absolutely nothing to apologize for. ''And how do you figure I have done that?''

How much of an idiot did he think she was? Emily wondered, as her chin angled up another notch. ''You knew all along you were going to meet her later tonight.''

"Really.'' Edmund gave her a condescending look as he continued to hold his ground. "And how did you deduce that?''

Easy. "By the fact you shaved and put on aftershave and silk pajama bottoms and brushed your teeth!'' Emily countered hotly, feeling frustrated and hurt beyond belief. He'd been getting ready for something and they both knew it.

Edmund regarded her with mounting impatience. "I did all that for you!'' he told her calmly.

"Me!'' Emily echoed disbelievingly, splaying both hands across her heart. His implacable certainty infuriated her even more.

"Yes, you.'' A heartbeat of silence fell between them, followed by another and another. "I did all that because I intended to make love to you tonight as soon as the kids were asleep and the lights were out. And you know what, Emily?'' he whispered seductively. "I still do.''

Chapter Eleven

Emily stared at Edmund, hardly able to believe her ears. "You can't be serious," she breathed. His profile was bathed in silvery moonlight, making him look more handsome, more determined, and more intent on making her his bride.

"Oh, but I am." He cupped her chin and brought her mouth up to his. With the mood between them, she expected a hot, dramatic explosion of physical passion, an ongoing extension of their argument, but instead he gave her a slow, gentle loving that turned her world upside down. Their embrace was brimming with emotion, filled with desire. Unable to resist his insistence, her arms moved from the defensive position against his chest, to wreathe around his neck. And still he kissed her, as if the chance would never come again, his lips moving over and over hers, until they parted helplessly and she was meeting him stroke for stroke, desire coursing through her veins with increasing heat. She felt his arousal pressing against her, demanding an intimacy she wasn't sure she would be wise to give. And she moaned softly in her throat, aware she was trembling from head to toe.

"Edmund—" she whispered.

"Hmmm?"

As his lips left hers and moved to the sensitive place just behind her ear, and his hands found her breasts and nimbly worked the nipples to aching crowns, she let out a soft, ragged sigh. "This wasn't what we agreed on when we decided to get married, Edmund," she said desperately as he unbuttoned her pajama top and bared her breasts to his heated gaze. Not that he was alone in his ardor. She wanted to see him, touch him everywhere, too.

He rained kisses down her neck, across her collarbone and the uppermost swell of her breasts. His lips traced a fiery erotic path as he bent to take her into his mouth, laving her breast with his tongue, blowing it dry with his breath. "When we made our agreement I hadn't kissed you yet."

But he was kissing her now, Emily thought, as everything around her blurred except for the hot, hard pressure of his mouth. The slow, hot, strokes of his tongue were unbearably sweet, unbearably sensual and fulfilling. The scent of his cologne filled her senses. And still he could not get close enough to her, nor she to him, she realized with a pleasure that was as alarming as it was exciting.

She moaned as he angled his body against her softness and his lips returned to hers. Arrows of fire shot through her, weakening her knees, making her cling to him as if he were the only life ring in a raging sea. Oh, dear. Edmund. "I don't...do this...just for fun."

"Then you should," Edmund teased as he tunneled both hands through her hair. He probed the soft, sensuous lining of her lips with his tongue, intoxicating her with his nearness and kissing her with a thoroughness she'd only imagined. "Because it can be," he whispered with an evocativeness that made her heart pound, "so much fun."

Giving her no more chance to protest, he swept her up into his arms and carried her to the bed. Reality gave way to fantasy as he lay her on the bed and stretched out beside her. Feelings took over. The next thing she knew their clothes were off and she was lying beside him. He swept his hands through the dark curls, caressing her dewy softness, moving up, in. Over and over, he stroked her, until she was arching against him, coming like lightning in his hands, her passion igniting his own.

"You see how it is with us?" he whispered as she shuddered beneath him uncontrollably, again and again. "It's proof we're meant to be together," he said as he shifted her so she was beneath him, his for the taking. "Proof that this should be a part of our lives, too."

Or proof, Emily thought, stunned by her wantonness, she was a naive fool. What was happening to her? she wondered, upset. She'd never been this way. Not with anyone! And while the idea of being his lover as well as his wife was as thrilling as it was exciting, allowing herself to be too romantic, to forget the practical side of things would be a big mistake. If she ever became steadily sexually involved with a man again, she wanted it to be an action born out of love, in a relationship destined to last a lifetime. Edmund had offered her a lot, but he had not offered her love. Worse, throwing sex into the mix could really mess up their friendship and their "platonic" arrangement. For their children's sake—for her own—she wanted this relationship to last.

Emily pushed away from him and said, "I can't do this."

Edmund blinked. Sat up. "Why not?" he demanded.

Because it happened for all the wrong reasons, Emily thought shakily. *Because I was jealous. You were angry.* And because she knew better. "Because I've seen this happen to other widows," Emily told him miserably, acutely aware there had been no words of love exchanged between them, and that she was not cut out for a quick, meaningless roll in the hay, no matter what her traitorous body might have been telling them both a few minutes ago.

Emily drew a deep breath as she struggled to cover herself with a sheet. "They have an impetuous, romantic involvement as they begin to come out of their grief. And then they're sorry. Because foolish liaisons with transitional others always end badly." She didn't want to be the object of desire Edmund used to help himself out of his grief, any more than she wanted to use him to accomplish the same objective. "And that goes double for those that are born out of mutual loneliness." And prior to her coming here, the two of them had been very lonely—their letters had been testimony to that.

He relaxed. Shook his head. "That's not what's happening to us," he said, as his probing gaze gentled. "I'm not your transitional other, I'm your husband."

In name only, Emily reminded herself gamely, as she flushed from head to toe. "Let me ask you this. Have you had other lovers since your wife died?" Emily demanded as she snatched up her pajamas and began tugging them on.

Edmund folded his hands behind his head and sat back. "Absolutely not."

Emily tore her gaze from his commanding arousal. "Well, neither have I," she said, her mouth dry.

"So?" he drawled, remaining where he was reclining on the bed.

"So—" Emily shot him a furious look and tried not to think about what he would feel like inside her "—that just proves what we were doing was born out of pent-up, purely physical need. It could've been anyone." Not true! her conscience shouted.

"Even Selena," she added jealously—and not quite accurately, her heart said. "If I hadn't come along and interrupted the two of you."

This time she'd gone too far. Edmund's face darkened angrily as he vaulted from the mussed covers of the bed and came to stand in front of her. "You're right. I could've had Selena tonight if I wanted her. I didn't. I wanted you, Emily."

"You feel that way now because of what nearly happened here tonight," Emily told him miserably, knowing in her head—if not her heart—that anything that had happened this fast couldn't be real.

"But will you feel that way tomorrow or next week?" And how would she react if he didn't? No, it was better to put an end to this mistake now, before either of them were any more hurt than they were already!

Edmund's lips tightened in frustration. He jammed his hands on his hips, his disappointment as palpable as the erection that just wasn't going to go away. "You don't have a lot of faith in me, do you?"

Deciding she should definitely look somewhere else, Emily looked down at her pajama top, and re-

alized she had buttoned it all wrong. Realizing she
didn't begin to have the manual dexterity at the moment to button it up right, she climbed into bed, sat
against the headboard, and pulled the covers up to her
chin. "I'm trying to be practical, Edmund," she told
him stubbornly, as she willed her arms and legs to
stop trembling.

Wanting this to be a real marriage did not make it
so, she reminded herself sternly, as she struggled to
get a grip on her spiraling emotions. She'd signed on
to be a nanny and mother to his daughter, and a friend
and platonic partner to him, and that was all. The
same went for him. They had an arrangement. A simple, painless arrangement. Love had not been anywhere in the equation.

Okay, so the ceremony, the rings, the playacting
for the sake of others had worked together to blur the
edges a bit, but the reality of the situation remained
the same. Take away the legal mumbo jumbo that
made them man and wife, or the circumstances that
had them living under the same roof, and for the moment, sleeping in the same bed, and all he was really
offering her was an affair. One that—given its quick,
loveless basis—probably wouldn't even last!

She drew a breath. "We rushed into the marriage.
I don't think we should rush into this, too."

Edmund climbed back into bed, too, as gloriously
naked and unashamed of his incredibly beautiful body
as she was inherently modest. "What we felt just now
is not going to go away or change, no matter how
much you analyze our actions, or how long you hold
me at arm's length, Emily," he insisted grimly.

She pushed away the guilt she felt, at leaving him
so...uncomfortable. It was nothing a cold shower

couldn't fix. And it was something he had known better than to start in the first place. She folded her arms in front of her.

"I still think it's a mistake, one I have no wish of repeating," she said.

"Fine."

"But, for the record," she added hastily, "I'm sorry I let things go as far as I did."

Edmund's sable brown eyes glowed with an ardent light.

"I'm not," he said softly. Then paused, and looked deep into her eyes, his desire as potent an aphrodisiac as the way he had kissed and caressed her. "I want you to remember how it felt to have me begin to make love to you. I want you to yearn for the rest. Because when we do finally come together, Emily, when we are finally joined as one, it's going to be spectacular."

SELENA APPROACHED Edmund at nine the next morning, as he was coming in the front door. Although she was as glamorously dressed as always, her smile was brittle around the edges. "Mr. and Mrs. King just left?"

"Yes." Even as they spoke, Edmund wondered what destructive scheme Selena was hatching now.

Selena walked slowly over to him. "Any decision from them yet?"

Edmund shook his head. "They've promised to let me know in forty-eight hours or less."

She looked at him, uncertainty in her eyes. "I hope Mr. and Mrs. King put King's Ransom here."

As long as they were baring their souls... "I hope you head back to Somerset Farm."

Selena regarded him with a sad, wistful smile. "I'm all packed."

"Good." Feeling they'd said everything they needed to say to each other the previous evening, he started to walk away. Selena caught up with him. Her expression determined, she placed her hand on his arm.

"Edmund. About last night—"

Oh hell, here they went again.

"I'm sorry I misread you."

Edmund shrugged and looked her straight in the eye. He was finished being polite out of habit. "No harm done."

Briefly, Selena looked crestfallen her striptease hadn't done more damage. She recovered quickly. "One more thing." Her hand tightened on his arm.

Edmund waited, curious as to what she was going to say or do next.

Selena licked her lips nervously. "I spent a fair amount of time yesterday afternoon entertaining the Bancrofts for your mother. It may interest you to know that they think Emily's had her sights on you all along. She wrote you all those letters in order to get you to feel sorry for her and then she married you for your money."

Emily had married him for his protection because they were in a common bind, because they'd both found single parenthood a lot sadder and lonelier than they'd expected. But none of that was any of Selena's business. Edmund flashed Selena a crocodile grin. "The farm is my inheritance, and the farm's in trouble," he said dryly, refusing to fall for her bait. "Or hadn't you heard?"

Selena flushed self-consciously. "Everyone knows

you'll do what you have to do to turn it around. In a year or two, Fairfax Farm will be as successful as ever. In the meantime, Emily and her son move from one socially prominent family to another.''

Selena spoke as if that were a bad thing, which was ironic, Edmund thought, since finding herself a socially prominent family to marry into was exactly what Selena was doing! Determined to have it out with Selena once and for all, Edmund plucked her hand from his arm and stared her down. "Our place in the social register is not what drew Emily here."

"Oh, I have no doubt she wants you, too," Selena said bitterly. "What woman wouldn't?"

Emily hadn't last night, and her rejection still hurt.

"I just think you should know she's using you," Selena continued vindictively.

For years, Edmund had felt sorry for Selena, and he'd felt a little guilty, too. He'd never meant to lead her on. He'd never wanted to hurt her. But it would have been so much kinder if he had been cruel. If he'd done so, she would never have held on to these unrealistic fantasies. She would've married someone else. Someone who might've been able to love her back in a way he never could.

"All right, that's enough." Edmund took her elbow and hustled her to the door.

Selena dug in her heels. "Edmund, for heaven's sake!" She struggled to be free of him. "What are you doing?"

"Helping you to the front door." Edmund pushed the words through his teeth.

Selena turned and clutched his arm. "I don't have my coat."

"Sorry," Edmund growled. "My oversight." He

yanked the luxurious fur from the front hall closet and tossed it none too gently around her shoulders. Jerking the door open, he was pleased to see the four-wheel drive farm Jeep in front of the steps, just as he'd ordered.

"My luggage—" Selena protested, flushing fiercely, as Edmund propelled her willy-nilly through the doorway.

"Not to worry. I'll see it's sent over to Somerset Farm directly. In the meantime—" Edmund forcibly ushered the blond beauty down the steps to the oldest and ricketiest farm vehicle they had. He gave her a boost into the front seat. "Have a nice ride home."

"This is so rude!" Selena fumed, drawing her fur around her.

Edmund had been hoping she'd think so. Over his shoulder, he said, "And do us all a favor, honey, and don't come back!"

EDMUND JOINED EMILY in their bedroom several minutes later. Just out of the shower, she had finished blow-drying her thick, wavy hair.

He shut the door behind him, ensuring their privacy, and strolled toward her. "Where are the kids?"

Acutely aware of both her nakedness beneath her robe, and what had almost happened between them the night before, she tucked the lapels closer to her breasts and tightened the belt at her waist. "They're downstairs in the sunroom with your mother, watching news coverage of the blizzard. Apparently, they are still looking for that runaway bride from Pennsylvania, Nora Hart Kingsley—she was last spotted driving in the mountains of West Virginia."

Edmund's heated glance covered her from head to

toe before he sauntered away from her and took a seat on the mussed covers of their bed. "I hope they find her."

Emily nodded, trying hard to ignore the way her heart was beating right now, or the edgy, incredibly alive way Edmund made her feel whenever he was around. "I do, too. West Virginia has been particularly hard hit by the blizzard and the people who saw her said she was still in her wedding gown."

She felt her breasts tightening beneath the soft flannel fabric of her robe, and saw that Edmund had noticed. But avoiding his appraisal Emily carried an ivory cashmere slacks and sweater set from her closet and hung them on a hook in the dressing area. "Was that Selena I just saw leaving?" Emily asked casually, trying hard not to show her relief about that.

Edmund lounged against the headboard and watched her select a lacy bra and panty set from her drawer. "Yes."

Both in hand, Emily flushed and stepped behind the screen. Aware her knees had that jittery, weak feeling in them again, she tossed her robe over the top and began to dress with hands that shook slightly. Finished, Emily stepped out. "Before that, the Kings?"

Knowing her hair was mussed from tugging her sweater on over her head, Emily went to the bathroom and picked up her brush, ran it through her hair.

"Right again," Edmund said. He pushed the edges of his jacket back, revealing a slim hip and a washboard-flat stomach.

"What are the chances you'll get their business?"

Edmund leaned back and clamped his hands over

the rock-hard solidness of his chest. "Hard to say. Maybe fifty-fifty."

Emily tried not to think about what he was doing to her senses. And he hadn't even touched her yet. "You don't look like you slept very well," she said calmly.

He cocked his head and gave her a thorough once-over. "You didn't, either."

Not surprising, since they'd both ended up clinging to their separate sides of the double bed. "Maybe having the house thinned out of company will help," Emily suggested.

"Maybe." The grim look was back in his sable brown eyes.

Emily swallowed around the sudden knot of tension in her throat. "Have you seen Whit and Andrea yet this morning?" She hadn't.

"They're still sleeping."

Emily had been hoping they would leave, too. Unfortunately, because they were Bobby's grandparents, she couldn't really kick them out. They had every right to see their grandson, too.

Emily paused and wet her lips. "I know you're as anxious to get rid of them as I am, but I wouldn't count on them leaving here any time soon—"

He lifted a mildly dissenting brow.

"Unless you march them off the premises, too," Emily said.

He pushed lazily to his feet and sauntered toward her. "You saw that?"

Emily stayed her place with effort. "It was hard not to, since I was looking out the window at the time."

He stopped just short of her, and stood towering

over her. "I asked her not to come back," he said softly.

The tension that had been plaguing Emily came back full force. "And if she does?"

Edmund looked down at her, the devil in his eyes. "Then I'll personally escort her off the premises again," he promised. "No one is coming between me and my wife," he told her, as his hands came up to cup her shoulders resolutely. "I don't care who they are, or how long they've been a friend of the family."

Emily turned away, her feelings in turmoil. Even though she was loath to admit it, Edmund had been right the night before. She was jealous. She didn't want him with another woman. She didn't want him with anyone but her. And she sensed that was not going to change.

Edmund circled in front of her, put his hands on her shoulders and let them slide halfway down her arms where they continued to cup her warmly. "And to that end, I think you and I need a new understanding between us, as well."

Emily's heart filled with hope as he bent to kiss her temple. "What kind of understanding?" she queried softly, aware more than ever, her life was taking on a fairy-tale quality whenever she was with him.

Edmund slid his arms around her back. He drew her close, so they were touching in one long electrified line. "I want to extend our original agreement to include absolute fidelity on both our parts." He tilted her face up to his and pressed a finger against her lips before she could interrupt. "I know you're not there yet," he said gruffly. "You made that very clear last night." He drew a breath then continued in a soft, urgent voice, "I just want you to know if and when you want to make love, that it has to be with me, and no one else." Framing her face with his hands, he forced her gaze up to his. "And the same goes for me. If I make love to anyone, it will be to you."

Desire trembled inside her, making her insides go all soft and syrupy. "That sounds fine," Emily said shakily as she splayed a hand against her chest, aware she had to be careful here not to promise more than she could deliver. She knew, of course, it was her fault they'd brought sex into this relationship at all—she didn't have to kiss him back that way or let them start to make love—but she still did not want to do anything the two of them would enjoy but later regret.

Edmund gave her a soft, sexy smile as his hands gently caressed her face. "I'm glad you agree."

Emily met his unabashedly ardent gaze head-on. "But I'm not making any promises that we will make love, either," she continued in a low, cautious tone. Not because she didn't want the physical closeness with him. She did, so very, very much. But because she knew that giving her body to him would also mean giving her heart and she couldn't do that unless she thought he could love her, too, in the same all-encompassing way.

To her stunned relief, he not only accepted her conditions, he understood her need to take things at a slower pace. "I'll wait for you, Emily. I'll wait however long it takes," he promised her with a solemn smile.

Looking into his eyes, she believed him.

"But just so you—and everyone else—will know how serious I am about making this hasty marriage of ours work," he told her in a low, confident voice,

"I'm giving you this." He drew a velvet box from his pocket. Inside was a diamond-and-sapphire engagement ring so beautiful it took her breath away.

"We might be getting into this relationship backward," Edmund continued huskily as he slipped it onto her finger, "but it doesn't mean the commitment I feel to you and our marriage is any less valid, or our future together any less bright." Holding tight to her hands, he lifted his head and looked deep into her eyes. "Every time you look at this, I want you to remember how much I want our marriage to work," he told her gruffly. "Not just as a convenience, Emily, or a better way to raise our kids, but as a real relationship, a real marriage and a real family."

Tears of happiness flooded her eyes. "Oh, Edmund—" Emily gasped softly.

Wrapping both arms around her, he brought her back into the safety and security of his arms. "This is for the future, Emily," he told her warmly. "This is for us." And he sealed the moment with a tender kiss.

"GUESS WHAT, Daddy?" Chloe told Edmund when he came up to the playroom to check on Emily and the kids later that day. "I finished an assignment in every subject this morning and Emily faxed them in to my teacher in Seattle for me."

Edmund smiled at his daughter as he reached over and affectionately ruffled her hair. He hadn't seen this much enthusiasm from Chloe in a long time. "Wow," he told his daughter seriously. "I'm impressed."

Chloe put down the blocks she and Bobby had been

playing with. "You know what that means, don't you? Show-and-tell with all four of us."

Emily met his eyes, belatedly securing permission. "If that's okay?"

"Sounds fun," Edmund said. Then he'd have to get back to work on the final details of the Fairfax Farm bid for King's Ransom, but right now, Edmund decided cheerfully, a time out with his new family was just what he needed.

"Who goes first?" Emily asked after they'd all seated themselves on the rug in the center of the room.

"You!" Chloe said enthusiastically.

Emily made a face. "We may have a problem, Houston," she quipped. "I haven't thought of anything yet."

Edmund was sympathetic to her plight. He was rusty at this, too.

"I'll help you," Chloe volunteered, scooting over to sit close to Emily on the floor. "Show-and-tell about your new ring." She pointed to Emily's delicate left hand.

Yes, Edmund thought, *tell me what you really think about the gift now that you've had time to consider the implications of it—the fact that I want you for my real wife and life partner and not just a mother-slash-nanny for my child.*

Emily looked down at the ring finger on her left hand, then held it out so everyone could admire it as much as she had when he'd first showed it to her. "Your daddy gave this to me this morning," she told the children proudly.

The question was, Edmund thought, had it been too much? Was he rushing her? If so, did she mind? Thus far, it didn't appear so. But he was all too aware his instincts about what a woman was really feeling and thinking were not the best.... He'd been blinded in the past, only seeing what he wanted to see. Whether he wanted to admit it or not, he knew it could easily happen again here, too. Especially with Emily, whose feelings toward him were still very new and fairly guarded.

Chloe peered down at Emily's ring. "It's very pretty," she said finally. "It really sparkles in the light." Chloe clasped her fingers together loosely, wrapped them around her knee, and turned to Edmund curiously. "How come you gave her a ring, Daddy?"

Because I'm falling in love with her, Edmund thought. But he couldn't say that in front of the kids, until he'd said it to Emily. And he couldn't do that until the time was right, until he knew in his heart she was ready to hear it from him. The problem was, he wasn't particularly good at reading women in general, and that shortcoming was even more pronounced with women he cared about.

"Because she's my wife now," Edmund told his daughter. He turned his gaze to Emily, lacing his low words with a meaning only she could catch. "And I wanted to give her something special, especially after all she's done for us."

Briefly, disappointment flickered in Emily's eyes. Before he could question her about it, Chloe looked at Bobby, who was waving his arms wildly and chattering away enthusiastically in baby talk. "It's too bad Bobby can't show-and-tell us something, too," Chloe remarked as Bobby stood carefully, then bobbed up and down in an attempt to walk solo. As they all watched, he lurched forward awkwardly, forgetting to pick up his feet as he moved. Thrown off balance, he fell forward on hands and knees. He looked frustrated at the failure, and about to cry. Edmund scooped Bobby into his arms. "Bobby and I'll do ours together."

Chloe grinned. "What are you going to do?"

Edmund angled a thumb at his chest. "I'm going to show-and-tell Bobby how to walk. See, little tyke, you stand up on your feet. Yeah. He's got that part down pat."

"It's the rest of it that's been giving him trouble," Emily said wryly.

"Now, watch carefully, Bobby." Edmund clamped a hand gently around Bobby's ankle, lifted his right foot, moved it forward and set it down. He repeated the action with the left foot, then went back to the right. "See? You're walking—almost all by yourself—and it's as simple as one-two-three."

When Bobby had the hang of that, Edmund held on to both of Bobby's hands, stood behind him, walked him to Chloe, then walked him to Emily, then back to Chloe and so forth. "You're doing great, my man," Edmund said.

But not great enough for his little charge.

"See if he can do it by himself now, Daddy!" Chloe demanded, about the same time as Bobby shook off Edmund's grip.

Edmund grinned at Emily. Bobby let out a rebel yell, bobbed up and down, lurched forward and once again forgot to move his feet. Geared for just such a contingency, Edmund caught him before he hit the ground. Thinking they were roughhousing, Bobby wriggled in Edmund's arms and giggled uproariously.

Chloe rested her chin on her fist. "Maybe he'll do it next time," she said, obviously disappointed. Bobby hadn't managed the feat alone.

"We have to be patient," Edmund told his daughter. Just as he planned to be patient for Emily and hoped her feelings mirrored his in time.

Emily nodded. "It's hard, I know. But when the time is right, it'll happen."

And so, Edmund hoped, would everything else. Because he wanted to dedicate himself to his marriage. Hopefully, as with all good investments, the endeavor would reap dividends of boundless love and happiness in the end.

"It's your turn, Chloe," Emily said.

Chloe jumped up and ran to get something from her backpack. "I have a picture. This is my class picture from my school back in Seattle." In great detail, she described her teacher and all her friends.

"Do you miss not being in school with other kids?" Emily asked gently.

"Sort of." Chloe fell silent as she struggled to put her feelings into words. "I thought it'd be different, doing my schoolwork at home. More fun, you know?

Edmund and Emily nodded.

"But instead it's just—sort of—"

"Lonely?" Emily guessed.

Chloe nodded. She turned to Edmund. "I kind of think I might want to go back to school again, Daddy."

"That would be fine," Edmund said. "But you know it can't be back in Seattle. It would have to be here in Kentucky."

"I know," Chloe said as she carefully displayed her class photo on a shelf, high above Bobby's reach, then returned to sit next to Emily. "Do you think I would make friends here?"

Emily smiled and gave Chloe a reassuring hug. "I think you'd make lots of friends."

Maureen appeared in the doorway. "There you four are! I wanted to tell you the plumber's here, working on the burst pipe in the cottage. He said it's fixable, although it's going to take a little time. You ought to be able to move back there late tomorrow."

"Thanks for letting us know," Edmund said.

Maureen nodded graciously, then turned to her granddaughter. "Chloe, you promised to help me select the menu for dinner this evening. Remember?"

"Right." Chloe turned to Edmund and Emily importantly. "I better go help Grandma Maureen."

As soon as they left, Edmund told Emily, "I guess she isn't going to be happy being home schooled after all."

Emily agreed. Her face lit with a maternal glow, she said, "She needs to be around other kids."

"You think she'll do better here?" Edmund didn't want to do anything that would create more difficulty for his daughter academically, especially when she had only really been able to concentrate on her classwork again for a couple of days.

Emily smiled and reassured him the way she'd just reassured his daughter. "It isn't going to be easy. She'll still have her up and down days, but with our love and support—"

Our love and support. Edmund liked the sound of that.

"Chloe really ought to do just fine."

"Is Daddy going to read me a story tonight or just come up and kiss me good-night?" Chloe asked cheerfully after she had gotten into her pajamas and brushed her teeth.

Emily helped Chloe unbraid her hair. "I'm sure he'll do whatever you want him to do."

Chloe had no trouble deciding what that was. "Both!"

Emily picked up Bobby, who was playing sleepily beside her. "Then let's go downstairs and get him."

"What's he doing anyway?" Chloe asked as the threesome stepped out into the upstairs hall.

"Working."

Chloe did a double take. "Still?"

Emily told herself his absence had nothing to do with the unslaked desire between the two of them. "He had phone calls to make to his clients in Seattle this afternoon and more farm business to take care of this evening."

"He's working too much!" Chloe grumbled, looking all the more unhappy.

"That's because he's trying to do two jobs now," Emily explained. And because the farm was in trouble. As soon as he got the farm business back on track, his life—and theirs—would be easier.

"Well, I don't like it," Chloe said as the three of them walked into the study.

"Don't like what?" Edmund asked, from behind the desk. He regarded his daughter, his brow furrowed in concern.

"Having you in here all the time," Chloe said, her lower lip taking a pouty thrust.

Edmund smiled and stretched, then stood and circled the desk. "Well, I don't like it, either." He wrapped his arm around his daughter and eyed Emily fondly, who still had Bobby settled on her hip. "Do you think I'm working too much, too?"

That was a loaded question if she'd ever heard one. Emily dropped her eyes from his sexy, searching gaze. "I understand you've had a lot to do," Emily said softly, glancing at the farm paperwork scattered across his desk.

Edmund sighed. "Unfortunately, it's liable to stay that way for a while."

"Do you have time to read me and Bobby a story?" Chloe asked.

"I always have time to read you and Bobby a story," Edmund said. "Do you have one picked out?"

Chloe shook her head. Edmund took her hand. "Then let's go upstairs and find one, shall we?"

Short minutes later, they were all comfortably ensconced in Chloe's room, on her bed. Watching Edmund read *Charlotte's Web* out loud, with she and the two children cuddled on either side of him, Emily was struck all over again by what a good, loving father he was, and what a great family the four of them made.

By the time he'd finished, Bobby was fast asleep, and Chloe was soon going to be. Emily tiptoed off to put Bobby to bed in the nursery. As soon as he was settled, she went back to kiss Chloe good-night. "I'm glad you're my mommy," Chloe said, as she reached up to hug Emily tight.

Emily hugged her newfound daughter back. "I'm glad you're my little girl, too," she said thickly.

"What about me?" Edmund clamped his hand over his head and pretended to be aggrieved.

"Oh, Daddy." Chloe giggled at his comical ex-

pression. "You know I love you, and Bobby, too!"
She reached up to hug Edmund fiercely and kiss him
good-night.

"See you in the morning, pumpkin," Edmund said.

"Okay, Daddy." They turned off the light and
slipped from the room.

Emily headed for their bedroom. Edmund was right
behind her. "You're not going back downstairs to
work?" Emily asked.

Edmund shook his head wearily, already taking off
his shirt and shucking his shoes, socks and pants. He
retrieved a pair of sweatpants from the drawer, and
pulled them on, then went into the bathroom to brush
his teeth. "I've about had it for tonight." He stuck
his head back out the door in time to see her gather
up her pajamas, too. "Where are Whit and Andrea?"

Blushing because she still wasn't used to living so
intimately with him, Emily stepped behind the screen
in the corner. "Last I heard, they planned to view
horse films with Gail and your mother," she told him
as she stripped off the discreet cranberry red wool
dress she'd worn to dinner. "Apparently," she said,
bending to kick off her pumps and strip off her panty
hose, too, "they've been so impressed with what
they've seen here the last two days they're thinking
of investing in a broodmare themselves, boarding and
breeding her here."

Her remark was greeted with utter silence. Unable
to resist getting a glimpse of him, she hurriedly
stripped off her bra and put on her pajama top and
bottoms, then stuck her head out from behind the
screen.

He was standing stock-still in the bathroom doorway, his arms folded across his bare chest. She

grinned at the carefully neutral expression on his face. "Just what you'd need, huh?" she teased, as she gathered up her discarded clothes with one hand and sauntered toward him.

Edmund shrugged. He watched as she hung up her dress in the closet and put her panty hose and bra aside for laundering. Following her lead, he dispensed with his daytime clothing, too. "I admit I've never cared for Whit and Andrea," he said, as he hung the suit he'd worn to dinner in the closet. "But, on the other hand," he said as he joined her in the bathroom while she brushed her teeth, "it would be good for Bobby to know his grandparents. Family's important."

"I agree," Emily said softly after she finished rinsing her mouth. She straightened, rolling her eyes. "Even if it does seem like they'll never leave."

Edmund followed her back into the bedroom. Pausing at the window, he frowned at the dark, cold, still night. "Do they know they're most likely going to get snowed in again tonight if round three of the blizzard hits us as hard as is predicted?"

Emily nodded. "They don't seem to care."

Edmund sighed as he went into the bathroom to brush his teeth. "Well, at least we got rid of Selena during the break in the weather this morning."

"Agreed."

Finished, he came back out, blotting his mouth with a towel. "You ready to turn out the lights?"

No, Emily thought, recalling the heated near-lovemaking they'd shared the previous evening in that bed, I'm not. She stepped back another pace, grabbed her terry cloth robe. "You go ahead. I need to check on Bobby one more time.'' And figure out how I'm going to deal with this.

He stepped toward the door, too. "I could do it."

"No. I'll go." She rushed past and felt only relief when he let her go. She was acting like a fool. Nothing was going to happen that she didn't want to happen.

Maybe that was the problem.

Because she did want to kiss him and hold him again. Even if she knew it wasn't wise.

Tiptoeing into her son's darkened bedroom, she noted Bobby was sound asleep. Still, she lingered, covering him with his blanket, going to get another.

And that was when she heard it. The heavy tread of male footsteps moving stealthily past in the hall. Those footsteps did not, however, sound like Edmund's. She stuck her head out in the hall, saw Whit Bancroft, clad in robe and slippers, too, tiptoeing toward the stairs, acting very much as if he did not want to be seen or heard.

Emily scowled. What in the world could her pesky former in-laws be up to now?

Chapter Twelve

Emily stood in the doorway of the study, watching Whit Bancroft riffle the papers Edmund had left on his desk. He'd always been presumptuous and self-serving, but this took the cake. "Just what do you think you're doing?" she demanded hotly.

Whit looked up, saw her and went right back to what he was doing. "Emily, this doesn't concern you."

Not sure whether she was more shocked or angered by the intrusion into Edmund's family's privacy, Emily sauntered over to the desk. "I think it does," she warned in a cold voice that let him know she was not going to permit him to get away with this!

Whit straightened with an exasperated sigh. "Don't you want to know what the financial condition of your new husband is?"

"Money's never meant anything to me and you know it."

"More's the pity."

Emily studied the pages in Whit's hands. "These are private Fairfax Farm records," she said in her coldest tone.

"Exactly."

Since it was clear he wasn't going to put them back of his own volition, she tried to wrest them away from him. "You've got no right to be going through them!" she warned as he won the tug of war.

Whit sat down behind Edmund's desk, and picking up where he'd left off, ran his finger down a column of numbers on the page. He quickly copied the number onto a paper. "Andrea and I are trying to protect you and Bobby!"

Emily grabbed paper and pencil the moment he let go of them. "Bobby and I don't need your protection, Whit," she said, quickly backing up out of reach, "and even if we did, this is not the way!"

Whit sat back in Edmund's chair. "Look, Andrea and I see nothing wrong with your trying to improve your lot in life however you can, in this case via marriage," he told her wearily. "It's something we all do."

No, Emily thought, it wasn't. "I did not marry your son to improve my lot in life, nor did I marry Edmund for his money or his position in life!" she said, pushing the words through her teeth. "I married them because I loved them and wanted to be with them. Both of them. And you know what?" she blurted out, before she could stop herself, or analyze the depth of feelings she'd just revealed. "That's okay!"

To her chagrin, Whit ignored her as he sized her up without the usual veil of upper-crust politeness. "But if you've chosen this path, and intend to stick to it—"

"I do!"

"Then you're going to have to do a lot better job of it."

Emily blinked. "Excuse me?"

"C'mon, Emily. Even you aren't that innocent!" Whit said, pulling his pipe out of his pocket. "You have to know that Bobby is in the way of your romance with your new husband."

"Bobby is never in the way!"

"Furthermore," he lectured, aiming his pipe in her direction, "you should be wearing silk, not flannel, nightwear. This is your honeymoon, for heaven's sake!"

Emily blinked. If he wasn't going to be polite, she wasn't going to make the effort, either. "Where do you get off talking to me this way?" she demanded.

Again, Whit ignored her. "To that end, Andrea and I could help you out, by taking Bobby off your hands for a little while."

He was acting as if Bobby were a nuisance to be dealt with! "For all our sakes, I'm going to forget you just said that," she told him tightly.

Whit closed the distance between them. "You're refusing the offer?"

"Hell, yes, I'm refusing." Emily leaned across the desk and snatched up the entire stack of Fairfax Farm papers in front of him. "Now get out of here before someone sees you."

He nodded at her coldly. "As you wish. But before I go I want you to know there is one thing Andrea and I haven't changed our minds about, and that's the trust Brian left to Bobby. We may not be able to win in a custody fight for Bobby now that you've married into such a fine family, but we are not going to let Edmund siphon money from it in the form of an investment for you to counter the recent farm losses here. We'll see Bobby's trust tied up in probate forever before that happens. And we have powerful lawyers who can do just that!''

His point made, Whit started to leave the study in a huff, then darted back inside.

Emily had only to look at his face to know something was up. ''What is it?'' she demanded.

In reply, Whit put a silencing finger to his lip, ducked behind the open study door. When she didn't move, he grabbed her wrist and jerked her back beside him, and it was at that instant, while she was still feeling pretty steamed herself, that Emily heard the voices coming down the hall. Maureen's first, raised as if in argument. ''...I don't see why you think it's a bad idea!''

Then Edmund, replying in kind. ''You should know better than to trust them an inch, Mother,'' Edmund was saying, in a low irritated tone. ''Never mind keep offering to let them stay here!''

Whit gave Emily a look as if to say, I told you so.

Maureen again: ''Gail says we need to do this, to demonstrate our willingness to include them in Bobby's life, should the custody case eventually come to court!''

Then Edmund again, even more irritated: ''Mother, don't be naive! They're here, gathering information to try to use against us! And you played right into their hands when you offered to try to do business with them. Don't you see how that will likely be portrayed in court? Like a shakedown in the form of 'You shore up our losses with your investment—we give you unlimited access to your grandson!'''

Whit nodded, as if that was exactly what was going to happen, and Emily's heart sank. What had she done, bringing all this grief to Edmund's doorstep?

"That isn't the way it was at all!" Maureen returned, sounding very hurt.

"I know that, Mother," Edmund continued, seeming all the more aggravated as they continued down the hall past the study, "but that's not to say a judge will."

"Look, son, I know you're still angry with me about trying so hard to pair you with Selena," Maureen said, as the footsteps abruptly came to a halt. "And I will be the first to admit I made a mistake. In the final analysis, she wasn't as kind and considerate a young woman as she has always seemed to be."

Edmund, who'd obviously stopped walking, too, made a rude sound. "That's an understatement if I ever heard one," he grumbled.

"But you don't have to continue this marriage to Emily just to get back at me!" Maureen fumed.

Beside Emily, Whit raised an interested brow.

"That's not what I'm doing!" Edmund retorted, sounding all the more incensed.

"Isn't it?" Maureen returned swiftly.

"I want to be married to Emily," Edmund declared.

Emily smiled victoriously at Whit as if to say, "Ha—so there!"

Maureen made a clucking sound of disapproval as beside Emily, Whit frowned, too.

"Because you love her?" Maureen demanded.

Emily held her breath, waiting for Edmund's reply, only to hear him declare tightly. "I'm not going to discuss this with you, Mother."

Once again, it was Whit's turn to appear victorious. The footsteps started again, receded down the hall, around the corner. "Now what do you say?" Whit whispered smugly.

Emily strode over to the desk, hastily tried to put the farm records back in the file from which they'd been taken. "I suggest you get out of here before they come back and catch you here, Whit."

"Catch you," said an ominously low, all-too-familiar voice, "doing what?"

At the sound of his voice, Edmund saw Emily jump a mile. Whit frowned. Both flushed with unmistakable guilt. Edmund continued on into the study.

"This really doesn't concern me," Whit said, rushing past them both. "Emily, I'll see you and Bobby in the morning." He shut the door behind him.

Enjoying the reversal of circumstances, Edmund lounged against the desk and folded his arms in front of him. "Well?"

"I know how it looks, but—" Emily flushed all the harder as she turned and put the sheaf of financial papers back on his desk "I can explain."

Oh, I'll just bet you can, Edmund thought, as he studied her increasingly uncomfortable expression. The question was: Should he let her talk her way out of it? Or give her a bit of a hard time, just for the heck of it?

Mischief sparkling in his eyes, Edmund thumbed through the papers in front of him. "I don't see why I should give you a chance to do so. After all," he reminded Emily, "you didn't give me much of a chance to explain when you caught me with Selena last night."

"That was different!" Emily huffed. She did not appreciate the way he was comparing the two situations. "Selena was standing there in the buff, declaring her undying devotion to you!"

"And you're in your pajamas and your former father-in-law just walked out of here wearing his."

Okay, so something could be made of that, if they'd been two different people, and she'd been completely immoral. Emily folded her arms in front of her, and wished she was still wearing a bra beneath her pajamas. "He wasn't trying to seduce me, if that's what you're implying."

"Glad to hear it." Edmund's glance drifted to her breasts, before returning to her face. "I'd still like to know why you were down here with Whit when you told me you were going to check on Bobby."

Emily swallowed around the sudden dryness in her throat. Forcing herself to remain calm and nonchalant, she explained, "I saw Whit tiptoe by Bobby's room. Instinct told me he was up to no good. I followed him downstairs, caught him going through your papers and demanded he get out of the study. Before I could get him to do so, we heard you and Maureen talking. He pushed me behind the door so you wouldn't see us when you went by." End of story. Or so she'd thought.

"If Whit was bothering you, you could have called out for help—I would have been only too happy to come to your rescue," Edmund suggested mildly.

Emily conceded the point to him with a slight dip of her head.

"So why didn't you?" Edmund persisted in a low, silky voice.

"I was embarrassed by Whit's ill-mannered behavior. Like it or not, it reflects on me, and I didn't want your mother to know about it."

He gave her a knowing half smile as he circled around the desk to her side. Still eyeing her with a depth of male speculation Emily found greatly disturbing, he shifted so he stood with his feet braced slightly apart. "And then there was the other component," Edmund insinuated dryly.

"That being?" Emily questioned loftily as her heart began to pound.

Edmund jammed his hands on his hips and narrowed his eyes. "That you were also interested in eavesdropping on what my mother and I were saying."

Emily turned on her heel and began to pace, her slippers moving soundlessly across the polished wooden floor. "I heard a little of it."

He caught her by the arm as she passed and tugged her forward until she collided with the hard muscles of his chest and abdomen. Sparks of electricity exploded at every point of contact. "And...?"

Emily's pulse pounded as she realized he looked as though he wanted nothing more than to stop talking and simply kiss her. "You're right in what you told her," Emily replied, pushing her own wish to kiss him aside. "Whit and Andrea are here to spy on all of us and hopefully dig up some dirt to use against us in court."

Edmund rested both palms on her shoulders. "So they still want custody of Bobby."

"As well as the million dollars Brian left in trust for Bobby," Emily confirmed.

Edmund frowned worriedly. "I told you before. My family and I'll do whatever it takes to help you keep custody of Bobby and get fiscal control of the money Brian left him. As Bobby's mother, you should have full access to that money now," Edmund told her sternly. "In fact, you should've had it all along."

Here was her chance to test him on this issue, Emily thought. To prove what Whit and Andrea were alleging was simply not true.

She looked up into Edmund's face. "Maybe I should just let the money go," she suggested softly. "Bobby doesn't really need it to live a happy life, and I wouldn't know what to do with that kind of money if I had it, anyway." Who knew? Maybe Whit and Andrea would even give up trying to get custody of Bobby if she gave the money up.

Edmund dropped his hands from her shoulders abruptly. He glanced out at the snowy night, turned back to her slowly and folded his arms in front of him. "Is that what you think Brian would've wanted—for you to turn the money he left Bobby over to his folks?"

Emily could feel the blood rushing to her cheeks even as she struggled to get a handle on her soaring emotions. "No. Brian turned his back on his parents' money when he went into teaching. But the trust money was from Brian's grandfather. He had intended to invest it for Bobby's education, health care, et cetera."

"Then that is what you should do," Edmund counseled her softly. He paused long enough to take a seat on the edge of the desk. "Who's handling the trust now?"

Emily swallowed, her adrenaline pumping for a completely different reason. She began to pace again. "It's still being managed by the Bancroft family lawyers, the same as always."

"What does your own attorney say?" Edmund persisted, intercepting her once again.

Emily flushed self-consciously. "I don't have one."

A light possessive grip on her arm, he pulled her near. "Why not?"

Again, Emily shrugged. Without warning, she had an idea what it would be like to be Edmund's wife in every respect, to wake up with him every morning, to lie in his arms every night. The knowledge was as tantalizing as it was unnerving. Being near him was like playing near a fire. Too far away, she'd never get warm. Too close, she'd get burned. Deciding it was best to keep a fairly pragmatic distance from him, she planted her hands on her hips and admitted, "I didn't know I needed one until a couple of days ago, since prior to that the subject of Bobby's custody had never come up."

Edmund's gaze narrowed. Suddenly, he was very still. "Is the trust fund still tied up in probate court?" he asked bluntly.

"Yes," Emily answered. "As far as I know."

Edmund nodded. Thought some more. Released a heavy sigh. "I understand wanting to walk away from financial problems—hoping they'll just go away," he told her eventually. "I've done the same thing about the farm." His lips compressed ruefully. "I've learned the hard way that only makes things more difficult in the long run."

"You think I need to take a more aggressive stand here," Emily guessed, feeling a little guilty she hadn't.

Edmund threaded his hands through her hair, pushing it away from her ears. Sliding his thumbs beneath her chin, he tilted her face up to his. "I think you need to be prepared to fight them tooth and nail, if it comes to that, and right now it looks like it will." He drew a breath and leaned closer in a drift of brisk, masculine cologne. The shadow of his evening beard clung to his face, making him look even more ruggedly handsome than usual. "As for the trust," Edmund continued, "I'll call them in the morning and find out exactly how tied up it really is."

He was offering to help her. She needed his expertise. So why was she still so vaguely uneasy? "And if we can get the trust through probate, what then?" Emily asked quietly. She angled a thumb at her chest. "I'm the executor. I meant it when I said I don't know much about investment strategy or money management." Especially when it came to such a huge amount.

"You don't have to worry about that." Edmund rubbed her shoulders reassuringly. "I'll help you keep watch over it and decide what to do with it. I'll even invest it for you, if that's what you want."

The seeds of doubt she'd been struggling against sprang to life once again. Emily turned her back to Edmund and felt her shoulders graze the hardness of his chest.

Edmund put his hands on her shoulders and turned her gently around to face him. His eyes softened as they searched her upturned face. "Look, Emily, I know the idea of managing the trust seems overwhelming, but it's what I do for a living."

"I know." Emily's chest and throat were so congested with emotion she could barely breathe.

"I'll help you figure out what to do with the money

when you get it, to optimize the best return," he promised mildly.

"You mean invest it," Emily said as her heart skipped several beats and her nerves frayed all the more.

"Yes, in something that's guaranteed to give you a good return, in something you can trust."

Emily looked down at the papers spread across his desk. Scattered among the financial statements for the farms and pages of figures scrawled with Edmund's writing, were sample ads, suitable for horse-racing magazines. "Did you ever figure out what you're going to do about the advertising budget for this year?" *Please, please, Emily prayed fervently, tell me you figured out a way to finance it.*

"No." Edmund frowned but did not take his eyes from hers. "I'm still working on that, along with myriad other problems concerning the farm." Giving her no chance to peruse them further, he gathered up all the papers, locked them away, then held out a hand to her. "But enough talk about the farm, and our troubles. Let's go upstairs."

"FEEL LIKE WE'VE done this before?" Edmund quipped, as they stood in front of the bedroom window, and watched the snow come down in thick white sheets.

Emily tried hard not to let the darkened bedroom, the proximity of the beckoning bed, or the memories of what had happened there the night before, unnerve her. It was, as she quickly discovered, pretty much a lost cause. All she could think about when confronted with the long, intimate hours ahead of them was the possibility of holding and kissing Edmund again.

She drew a breath as he gallantly helped her slip off her robe. One less layer of clothing between them. "When did it start?" she asked, irritated by the telltale breathlessness in her voice. "Do you know?"

"It can't have been very long ago," Edmund guessed, wrapping his arms around her and bringing her back to rest against his chest. "Maybe thirty minutes?"

She turned to face him, her flannel-clad legs brushing against his gray-jersey-clad ones. "This does not look good, in terms of getting rid of the rest of the houseguests," she joked. Nor did it particularly bode well for the still not completely repaired plumbing in the cottage.

Edmund tightened both his arms about her waist and gathered her close, until the warmth emanating from his tall, muscled body beckoned to her like a soft, cozy feather bed.

He also did not seem to mind being snowed in. "The kids will enjoy it, though," he whispered against her ear.

"Yes, they will."

The silence stretched out awkwardly. He lifted a hand to her hair and sifted through the silky strands. "Everything okay?" he asked, the concern in his voice fueling her own.

Emily took a deep breath. It was and it wasn't. She finally had a man in her life again. Only the facts were less certain. Aware he was waiting for an answer, she ducked her head and said, "I'm just worried, I guess."

"You don't have to be," he told her as he continued to stroke her hair and hold her close. "I'll always be here to protect and care for you the way a husband should.''

But did he love her? Could he? Emily knew, better than most, that there were no guarantees about what the future held. They had today. Tonight. They had this moment in their marriage. A moment that might never come again. And suddenly she knew what she had to do. She shifted against him restlessly. ''Edmund?''

''Hm?''

Throwing caution—and innuendo—to the wind, she wreathed her arms about his neck, and aligned all of her against all of him. ''Kiss me,'' Emily pleaded softly, knowing if there was any way to take their marriage to a stage where no one—not Selena, not the Bancrofts, not Maureen, nor court battles or discussions of money—could interfere with it, where their hearts and souls blended as one, this was it.

Emily lifted her lips to his and set them perfectly beneath his. ''Kiss me,'' she repeated softly, sensually, ''the way you did last night.''

Edmund tensed but did not let go of her. ''Considering the way things ended,'' he told her gruffly, ''I'm not sure that's such a good idea.''

Had she not already been head over heels in love with him, Emily wouldn't have thought it a good idea, either. But the indisputable truth was she did love him, and he felt so good against her, so warm and strong and solid. As long as he held her, she felt nothing and no one could hurt her. As Emily gazed up into his face, she knew she wanted him to feel the same peace.

''They won't end the same way tonight,'' Emily reassured, knowing she had never wanted like this, never ached so just to be touched, loved, held by a man. But it wasn't just any man she wanted. It was Edmund.

Trembling with pent-up desire, he stared down at her, the implacable look back in his eyes. "What are you saying?"

Emily took a deep breath as another torrent of need swept through her. "That I want to make love to you tonight."

EMILY HAD SURPRISED him from the get go. But this, Edmund thought, as he stared down at her, beat absolutely everything. "You're sure?" he asked huskily, aware he had never wanted a woman the way he wanted his wife tonight.

Emily snuggled closer, her lips moving against his throat. "More certain than of anything in my life."

Edmund swallowed. He was finished rushing her into anything. That way only led to disaster. "Last night—"

"I was afraid to make this a real relationship and a real marriage." Emily touched a fingertip to his lips and looked deep into his eyes. "I'm not, anymore," she told him with a sweet, solemnness that tore at his soul. "To heck with all the forces trying to pull us apart."

Ditto that.

"I want to be your lover, Edmund. I want to be your partner and your wife."

"Well, in that case—" Edmund slowly, sensually backed her up against the wall, putting his arms on either side of her, his body against hers "—I say—" he whispered tenderly as he leaned over and lowered his mouth to hers "—we get started."

Holding her tightly, he embarked on a languorous kiss that gave way to a shower of hot, passionate kisses. Her response was immediate and volatile. She grabbed his arms, digging into his biceps and melting against him, and he reveled in it. Reveled in the hot, insistent demand of her body, and the sweet, womanly sweep of her tongue. Her kiss was minty, acquiescent and wonderful.

Aware he hadn't begun to have his fill of her, Edmund swept her up into his arms and carried her to the bed. Focusing on the unabashedly ardent promise in her eyes, he followed her down onto the sheets and stretched out beside her. Feeling her begin to tremble even more, he began to unbutton her pajama top. A shudder ran through her as he bared her rose-tipped nipples and creamy breasts to his rapacious gaze. Before he could take one in his mouth, she gasped and groaned. Then put a hand up to stop him and shifted so she was no longer beneath him. "Um—no, Edmund."

So hungry for her he could hardly bear it, Edmund rolled onto his back, his breath coming hard and fast. "No?" What did she mean "no" when she was looking at him with such uncompromising longing in her eyes?

"It's my turn." She fit her hand shyly to the hard ridge of arousal in his pants, and gently caressed the edge. That much was enough to threaten to push him over the edge.

Edmund groaned as her hands learned every male inch of him, then moved to the smooth, velvety hardness, and the depth of his need. A need she had created, and could ease. "Emily..." His hand closed over hers, holding her against him.

His other hand cupped the back of her neck, and he brought her mouth down to his once again, his lips covering hers until she felt and returned every ragged edge of his need. When she moaned soft and low in her throat, when her breasts peaked beneath his hands, and his hardness doubled in her hands, he drew back to look at her once again. Still clad in her pajamas, she swung herself over top of him, the insides of both her thighs cupping the outside of his hips.

"Just who is seducing whom here?" he demanded on a brusque, uneven note.

While one hand dipped beneath the waistband of his pants, her other hand trailed beneath the hem of his T-shirt across his chest. She grinned as she divested him of his clothes. "I'll let you guess," Emily said, as her lips headed further south, lingering first over his flat male nipples, before arrowing down to the indentation of his navel. He sucked in a ragged breath. "I think...I'm beginning...to get the idea." And then some.

"Good." The silk of Emily's hair whispered over his thighs as she leaned forward to touch him with the tip of her tongue. "I think you're going to like this even better." Determined to give him the pleasure he had given her, she adored him over and over, until he trembled with the need to hold back his own release.

Hooking both hands around her waist, he brought her back up. He kissed her mouth thoroughly, in a slow, hot mating dance. "Time to switch places."

Her eyes were lively with the combination of laughter and passion. "I wasn't finished," she told him playfully as she reached for him again.

Edmund groaned as he quickly undressed her. He

knew it would take very little to send him over the edge. When that happened, he wanted to be deep inside her. "Yes," Edmund teased right back as he paused to kiss her thoroughly again. "You were." He shifted her onto her back, and slid between her knees. The V of her thighs cradled his hardness and his sex throbbed against her surrendering softness.

"But I was making up for last night."

Aware there was no longer any question about what she wanted or what was coming next, Edmund fit his lips around the tip of her breast and sucked lightly, until she strained against him. "Trust me," he said, as he kissed her repeatedly with languid kisses that were every bit as intimate as his caresses. "You've more than made up for it."

Emily sighed wistfully as he wrapped her in his arms and pressed his lips into the fragrant softness of her hair. "You think?"

He loved her with his mouth and hands and tongue until she moaned softly in her throat and her back arched off the bed. "I think." He went lower still, wanting, needing to kiss her in the most intimate way.

"Edmund!"

"Play fair now." He explored her inner thighs until she trembled. "It's my turn." He went down to her knees and slowly worked his way back up again.

"I'll say."

"Like that, hm?" He pressed butterfly kisses into her center while his fingers slid deep inside her.

Emily gasped and trembled. "Very much."

"Good." Edmund grinned as he slid back up her body. "Because I plan on doing this often." He stroked her dewy softness, moving up, in. She surrendered helplessly.

"You do." Her tongue swept along his, circling, moving past the edges of his teeth before dipping deep. Soon they were kissing hungrily again, until he no longer knew where her mouth ended and his began. "Now?" Emily whispered softly, as her hands caressed his chest. She moved her hips impatiently, rubbing against him, into him, until he was shuddering, too.

"Now," he agreed. He moved between her legs, sliding his hands beneath her, nudging her thighs wider. She opened herself up to him as gently and irrevocably as a flower blooms in the spring. He surged forward. And then they were one.

He loved her an inch at a time, going deeper and deeper. With an exultant cry, she closed around the hot hard length of him. Trembling, they moved together, loving each other with every fiber of their beings, connecting with each other as one. And when they had finished, when they were wrapped in each other's arms and still holding each other very tight, the snow was still coming down.

Chapter Thirteen

About making love to Emily, about making her his wife, Edmund had only one regret.

With another six inches of snow on the ground, and Bobby and Chloe both waking at the crack of dawn, there hadn't been enough time for them to sort things out between them, or discuss the change in their relationship this morning.

But that would come in short order, he told himself firmly, as he paced his study, quaffed his coffee, and caught a glance of the thick new layer of additional snow blanketing all the trees. He'd make Emily understand that what had happened between them had not been an outcropping of simple desire, but a sign that their relationship was meant to be—*and* the consummation of their marriage.

They were officially man and wife now. And nothing was going to tear them apart. Nothing.

Without warning, Chloe appeared in the doorway to his study. She was dressed to the max in cold weather gear.

"Come outside in the snow with us, Daddy!" Chloe invited with her customary exuberance as she stomped in, boots and all. "Aunt Gail and Emily and me are gonna take Bobby sledding again! We're even gonna build another snowman! See?'' Chloe pulled a plastic bag containing a carrot, two radishes and a curving red pepper slice from the pocket of her down jacket. ''We've got veggies to make a face!''

Edmund grinned. ''That is cool,'' he enthused.

''But you're not coming, are you?'' Chloe guessed out loud, effectively bringing him right back to the present.

''Not right now,'' Edmund conceded reluctantly as he reached down and affectionately ruffled his daughter's hair.

Chloe's face fell.

Bobby bounced up and down beside her while Emily knelt in front of him, fastening the Velcro tabs on his snow boots.

''I suspect your daddy has important business to attend to this morning,'' Emily told Chloe gently as she set Bobby on his feet and straightened, too. ''Am I right?''

Edmund nodded. *More than she knew.*

He looked back at Chloe. ''I'll try to join you later, pumpkin, okay?''

''Okay, Daddy. Just don't wait too long,'' Chloe said, as she glanced out the window and saw Gail coming up the sidewalk with the sleds. ''We don't want you to miss out on *all* the fun.''

''I certainly wouldn't want to do that,'' Edmund drawled.

Emily looked up at him and grinned. Edmund leaned down to whisper in her ear, ''I know what you're thinking about. The same thing I'm thinking about. Last night.''

Emily sighed contentedly. "It was wonderful, wasn't it?"

He nodded. More so than anything he'd ever dreamed. "You bet it was." He brushed a tender kiss on her temple. "And it's going to be again." *Just as soon as he got this business with the Bancrofts taken care of.*

Emily kissed his jaw, just below his ear. "Tonight?"

It was Edmund's turn to grin. "Or sooner," he promised softly as an impatient Gail beckoned them outside.

Edmund held the door for Emily and the kids, promised to join them as soon as he could, then went to the study and shut and locked the doors behind him. Picking up the private line, he dialed the phone number of the law firm handling the trust for Bobby. A short but disturbing conversation later, he had all the information he needed.

"SOMETHING'S HAPPENED between you and my brother, hasn't it?" Gail said, watching along with Emily as Chloe took a turn giving Bobby a ride in the toddler snow sled.

Emily put the finishing touches on the snowman the four of them had built together. "What do you mean?"

"I mean it's become a real marriage instead of a means to an end."

Emily turned to Gail, blushing. She hadn't expected to make love with Edmund last night, but was she glad they had, for suddenly it felt as if she had her whole life ahead of her again. It felt as if the future were going to be terrific. "It's that obvious?" Emily murmured happily.

"Oh, yeah." Gail sighed wistfully. "You two look like a couple of lovebirds."

The only problem being, Emily thought, that neither of them had once mentioned love in the night. But she supposed that would come for Edmund, in time. At least she hoped it would. As for herself—she already felt it deep in her heart and knew now that she always would.

"Hey! Here comes Daddy!" Chloe shouted.

Emily turned. Sure enough, Edmund was walking out the back door of the mansion. Clad in a cashmere sweater, casual wool slacks and a down-filled outdoor sport jacket, he looked more handsome than ever. But, surprisingly, not quite as happy and relaxed as he had earlier, either.

Immediately, Emily tensed. Was something wrong? Had something happened? Or was her imagination working overtime?

"Daddy, you gotta come see our snowman!" Chloe shouted excitedly as she dragged the toddler sled over to Emily, handed the reins and Bobby over to her, then took off for Edmund.

Bobby, seeing Edmund, immediately gripped the rails, used them as leverage to push himself up, and scrambled to his feet.

"Whoa, there, hon," Emily said, reaching down to lift her baby son up and out of the sled. "Let Mommy help you."

"No!" Bobby said with surprising vehemence. While Chloe was engulfing her dad in a big hug, then taking him by the hand and dragging him toward the snowman, Bobby began grunting in frustration and squirming to get down. Figuring he wanted to touch the snowman too, Emily gently set him down next to it. Again, he resisted her attempts to hold on to him.

"I think he wants to practice standing on his own again," Edmund said, smiling and kneeling down in front of Bobby and the snowman.

"I think you're right," Emily said, smiling.

"Look, he's doing it!" Chloe said, excited as Bobby held both hands out for balance and stood in front of Edmund, unassisted. "He's standing all by himself, everybody!"

"He sure is," Gail murmured, grinning too.

Then Bobby surprised them all by lifting a booted foot ever so slightly off the snow. A hilarious expression on his face, he wobbled a moment from side to side while everyone held their breath. Then awkwardly put it down in front of him, lifted the other and put it down, too.

"Did you see that, Daddy? Bobby walked! He took a step!" Chloe shouted, as tears of joy streamed down Emily's face.

His eyes glistening with parental pride, too, Edmund held out his hands. "C'mon, little man, you can do it," Edmund coaxed gently. "You can come all the way to me."

His expression one of intent concentration, Bobby did just that, stepping first right, then left, then right again.

"My gosh, I don't believe it…three…four…five!" Gail counted, as proudly as any aunt, as Bobby toddled right into Edmund's arms, let out a warrior's cry and threw his arms around Edmund's neck. And then he did it again—he amazed them all, by speaking to

Edmund just as his "big sister" Chloe did. "Daddy," he said. *"Daddy."*

"YOU SHOULD'VE SEEN IT, Grandma Maureen," Chloe recounted breathlessly half an hour later, as they all enjoyed cocoa and toast in the kitchen while they warmed up. "Everyone was crying—even me!"

Maureen dabbed her suspiciously moist eyes. "Sounds like there wasn't a dry eye in the house," she remarked in a choked voice.

"Even now," Edmund quipped wryly, still feeling both overcome with emotion and amused himself. Daddy. Bobby had actually called him Daddy. Edmund knew it had only been a matter of days, but Bobby had become a son to him. He knew Brian wouldn't have minded, any more than he would if the situation were reversed.

"Well, I always knew he could do it," Chloe continued bragging proudly, as any big sister might. "I just didn't think it'd be in the snow! You're a real snow baby, aren't you, Bobby?" she teased.

To which Bobby replied in a string of indecipherable baby talk that made everyone laugh and clap appreciatively all over again.

Mrs. Hamilton, their housekeeper, appeared in the door. "Edmund? Whit and Andrea are waiting for you in the study, just as you asked."

Abruptly, all eyes turned to Edmund curiously. Knowing it was time this was taken care of, he stood. "Gail, if you and Mother will watch the kids, Emily and I have some business to take care of with the Bancrofts."

Emily blinked. "We do?"

"We do."

"Of course we'll watch the kids," Gail said.

Maureen nodded. "I want to hear more about this snowman you built. Where did you come up with the idea to use radishes for eyes...?"

Emily and Edmund fell in beside each other. "What's going on?" Emily asked, as they walked down the hall.

I'm in love with you, Edmund thought, as he took her hand in his. *Head over heels in love with you.* "I think I found a way to settle things with Whit and Andrea." And as they neared the study where the Bancrofts were waiting, he filled her in.

"YOU HAD NO RIGHT talking to our attorney about the trust!" Whit Bancroft fumed as soon as Edmund revealed the reason for the meeting.

"And you had no right forging Emily's signature on those power of attorney papers!" Edmund replied.

"What's he talking about?" Whit demanded tersely of his wife.

"I'm sure I wouldn't know," Andrea retorted, flushing.

"Then I'll be sure to explain it to you," Edmund said in a voice dripping with sarcasm for he and Emily now knew Whit and Andrea were both in on this up to their eyebrows. "The trust has not been—as you've told Emily all along—'tied up in probate court.'"

"Then why hasn't Emily had access to it?" Whit demanded.

Playing out the game to the bitter end. Edmund glared at the Bancrofts. "Thanks to the forged power of attorney bearing Emily's name, control of it was handed over to you two months ago. But that's not all.''

"It's not?" Andrea said, as she and her husband anxiously continued to play dumb.

"Four hundred thousand dollars has been withdrawn. Now," Edmund continued in a deceptively smooth, deferential tone, "if you want me to call in your attorneys—who erroneously thought Emily was too distraught to come into their offices personally to sign the power of attorney papers—and the police about this theft I will."

"That's not necessary," Whit said stiffly. He looked at Emily cooly. "I admit my wife and I took matters into our own hands."

"You mean you robbed Emily and your grandson of their money."

"No," Whit corrected authoritatively, "I mean we *borrowed* some of the trust funds." He took out his pipe and began filling it with tobacco from his pouch. "We fully intend to put it all back."

"Oh, you're going to do that, all right," Edmund agreed. "And you're going to do it ASAP."

Andrea looked at Emily with an air that was both haughty and assuming. "You can see now why we didn't want to turn over the trust to you at this time," Andrea explained, as if it were the most natural thing in the world. "We needed to recoup the money we borrowed."

"And how were you planning to do that?" Emily asked dryly, wanting to shoot herself for her naïveté where her in-laws and their personal financial matters were concerned. She should have known all along it was money at the heart of the custody battle, not her son!

"I'm glad you asked," Whit said. Cupping one hand over the end, he paused to light his pipe. "Andrea and I have been presented with a unique opportunity to invest in a start-up company that's going to sell computers on the Internet. All we need to jump in is five hundred thousand dollars—"

Five hundred thousand dollars. Or half of Bobby's trust fund. "Take it from me. It's never wise to bet the farm," Edmund advised.

Whit blinked. Apparently, it hadn't occurred to him they wouldn't eventually get their way on this. "But—"

"No buts," Edmund said, as he held up a silencing hand. "Now, because you're family, Emily and I have decided to go easy on you. So here's what you two are going to do. You're going to sell whatever you need to sell of your own assets to recoup the four hundred thousand dollars you borrowed from Emily and Bobby without permission. Then you are going to drop all efforts to gain custody of your grandson and sign legal papers advising your own attorneys what you have done so the trust will go back to Emily's control once again. Otherwise, Emily and I will have no choice but to seek criminal prosecution against you two for theft."

Silence fell in the room. The Bancrofts looked at Emily and Edmund, then each other. "Well..." Andrea sighed.

"We certainly don't want that," Whit agreed.

Edmund took Emily's hand and held it tightly. "Furthermore, since every child should have grandparents to dote on him or her, you two will be able to see Bobby whenever you want, just as Brian would've wished, but you will do so here, under Emily's supervision. No other way, no other place. Is this clear?''

"Very." Whit drew on his pipe as the rich scent of tobacco filled the room.

"Good." Edmund headed for his desk. He picked up the phone and began to dial. "Now, while we're still on the same page, let's make that call to your attorneys so you two can tell them what you've done."

What followed was a tense conversation, via one speakerphone to another, but thanks to the use of the fax in Edmund's study, an hour later, all had been resolved, verbally and in writing.

Breathing a huge sigh of relief they weren't going to jail for what they'd done, Whit and Andrea thanked Maureen for her hospitality, said goodbye to Bobby and took off via taxi on the just-cleared country roads.

Edmund and Emily watched until they were out of sight. She turned to Edmund. "I have a feeling they won't return often," she said, as she struggled with her mingled feelings of sadness, disappointment and relief.

"I suspect that will be the case, too," Edmund confided as he wrapped her in the warmth and security of his arms. "Nevertheless, I think they do love Bobby in their own way."

Emily sighed and rested her head against his shoulder. "I do, too." She paused, then tightened her arms around him and lifted her head. "Have I thanked you for helping me put an end to this dilemma?"

Edmund stroked her back with long soothing motions. "You just did." He bent his head to give her a long, exceptionally thorough, exceptionally gentle kiss.

Emily sighed contentedly as they drew apart. "My problem's solved," she told him cheerfully. "Only yours to go."

"Don't worry," Edmund grinned, refusing to let anything bring them down. "We'll handle it together."

BUT, WAS IT FAIR? Emily wondered, as she put Bobby to sleep for his afternoon nap, and Edmund went back to crunching numbers and working on coming up with an advertising budget in the study. Edmund had gone out on a limb to help her. Shouldn't she be doing more to help him than simply acting as head cheerleader?

Settling Chloe with Mrs. Hamilton in the kitchen, she headed for the solarium to talk to Maureen. And that was when she heard it—the sound of Maureen, doing in her own son.

"...well, of course I've tried my best...but I'm no businessperson. I helped, all those years, but it was Edmund's father who ran the farm and managed the business. I simply handled the entertaining. The social graces. Things can still and will turn around, of course. Now that Edmund has decided to stay on and help out...."

Emily backed out of the solarium, without having been seen. Heart and mind racing, she backtracked down the hall. So much made sense now. No wonder customers had lost faith in the farm. If Maureen didn't believe she could run the family business alone, if she didn't believe things were as good as they could or should be, how could anyone else be expected to, either? But she couldn't go to Edmund with wild speculation. She needed proof of what had been happening, and why.

An hour and half a dozen phone calls later, Emily had it.

Arranging for Mrs. Hamilton to keep an eye on Bobby for a while, she went to the study to talk to Edmund.

He leaned back in his chair as she swept toward him, and gave her a once-over that had her heart racing even before he pulled her down onto his lap. "So?" The pleasure he felt at seeing her again was in his low, sexy voice. "To what do I owe this honor?"

Emily drew a deep, bracing breath, wishing she didn't have to be the one to tell him. "I've got some good news and some bad news. Which do you want first?"

Abruptly, Edmund's mood became as careful as hers. "How about the bad?" he asked gravely, a hint of worry in his sable brown eyes.

Emily explained what she had overheard, then went on quickly to tell him what she had done about it. "I talked to Gail, who gave me a list of people who had recently withdrawn business from the farm. I called them and talked to them, told them we had recently married, and were very interested in seeing the farm do well again. Without exception, every client—including the Thurstons—eventually admitted it was your mother's lack of confidence in her ability to run things here that engendered their own lack of confidence in Fairfax Farm." The bad news over, Emily rushed on. "The good news is they all said if you returned permanently and took over day-to-day operations—as you now plan to do— they'd have no trouble returning their business pronto.''

The gamut of emotions was in his eyes. ''That is good news,'' Edmund said quietly. He looked over at her, telegraphed his thanks, and then sighed as worry permeated his handsome features once again. ''Now all we have to do is hope Mr. and Mrs. King say yes to the idea of Fairfax Farm being King's Ransom's new home.''

That would solve so many problems, Emily knew. Nevertheless, she had confidence Edmund could rebuild the farm to a level that surpassed its former glory as one of the finest in all Kentucky, whether they snared the famed stallion or not.

She wreathed her arms around his neck and snuggled close, wishing she could speed up the resolution of this problem for him, too.

Her teeth sliced into her lower lip. ''I don't know if I can wait another twenty-four hours to find out what the Kings' decision is going to be.'' She wanted Edmund to win this bidding war so badly!

Edmund studied the delicate U of her collarbone. ''Oh, I imagine we'll think of some things to do,'' he teased, as he bent to kiss her throat, then her cheek, her temple, before finally settling on her lips with ardent intensity. ''I know I've already got a number of good ideas.''

And, Emily thought dreamily as he continued to kiss her and hold her and make love to her as if they had all the time in the world to be together, what good ideas they were.

"OH, NO!" Chloe said later that evening as the four of them settled down to watch a family show together after a cozy dinner with just Maureen and Gail.

"What is it, honey?" Emily asked immediately, concerned by the outright worry she heard in Chloe's voice, at the end of the newsbreak.

Chloe dropped the crayon she'd been coloring with onto the page of her activity book. "Didn't you two hear that? The news guy just announced they're re-opening all the schools in Kentucky tomorrow, now that the roads are clear."

Beside Emily, Edmund shrugged. "Great," he said. "Or not so great?" He paused, studying his daughter's face. "What's the matter, honey?"

Chloe shot an apprehensive look at Emily. She picked up her crayon again and began twisting it between her fingers. "I know I said I wanted to enroll in school here."

"I remember," Emily said gently.

Chloe swallowed. She jumped up and started to pace. "But now I'm not so sure. I mean, what if the kids don't like me? What if it's too different from my old school back in Seattle? What if—?"

"Whoa, now," Emily interrupted, putting up a hand to stop Chloe before she could get any more wound up. "I think you're letting the cart get ahead of the horse here." She knew from her years of teaching third grade that the first thing Chloe needed was to feel she was in command of her own destiny. The second was the ability to make a choice or two of her own. And though she couldn't do anything about the move from Seattle to Kentucky, she did have a say in what happened here. "First of all," Emily said gently, praying Edmund would see where she was going and back her up on this, "you don't have to go to Sweet Briar Elementary School if it's not to your liking.''

Chloe blinked in surprise while Edmund looked equally intrigued. ''I don't?'' Chloe gasped.

''No. I'm sure there are a number of public and private schools here that are all excellent, right Edmund?'' She met his eyes.

''Right,'' Edmund said firmly, as he reached over to squeeze Emily's hand, letting her know with that simple gesture that he trusted her enough to give her free rein.

''And just because Sweet Briar Elementary School was right for your daddy doesn't mean it's going to be right for you,'' Emily continued to soothe Chloe as Chloe came up to sit between Emily and Edmund on the sofa. ''But, I think we ought to at least visit it and a few others while we're at it, sort of check them out. Don't you?''

''You mean you'd take me?'' Chloe asked, as a drowsily content Bobby situated himself even more comfortably on Edmund's lap.

Emily nodded. ''If it's okay with your daddy, sure.''

Chloe turned to him, her anxiety fading gradually as anticipation took its place. ''Daddy? Is it okay?''

Edmund grinned. ''I think that'd be a great idea, pumpkin. After all, Emily's a teacher and she probably knows a lot more about how to check out a school than I do.''

''But what if I don't like any of the schools we visit, Emily? What then?'' Chloe asked plaintively.

''Then you can continue to be taught at home by me. We can set up a schoolroom here, and a regular schedule for you to do your work. It's a process called home schooling. But, on the other hand, you might have been right yesterday when you said it was no fun doing schoolwork if you didn't have any other kids doing schoolwork with you. I mean, it's okay for a couple of days if you're on a trip or if you're sick and can't get to school, but most of the time kids your age like to be around other kids your age. Otherwise they get too lonely, right?''

''Right.'' Chloe shifted over onto Emily's lap and cuddled close. Her mouth formed a thin, tense line. ''So, does this mean we get to go look at schools tomorrow?'' she asked, looking up at Emily with equal parts of hope and dread. ''Just you and me?''

Emily smoothed her hair as a short, taut silence fell. As much as she wanted to mother Chloe, she didn't want to usurp Edmund's place. ''You don't want your daddy to go with you?'' she asked gently.

Chloe exchanged glances with her dad then shook her head solemnly. ''I think this is something just a mom and her little girl should do, don't you?''

A mom and her little girl. Realizing Chloe thought of her as a mother brought a lump to Emily's throat and an answering fullness to her heart.

''Daddy,'' Chloe decided firmly, as the tightness around her mouth and eyes eased, ''can come along later.''

''I DIDN'T MEAN TO cut you out of the school selection process,'' Emily said, as she and Edmund prepared for bed later that same evening.

Edmund wrapped his arms around her waist, drew her back against him, and pressed his lips to the exposed column of her throat. ''You didn't.''

Shivers of desire swept through her. Emily closed

her eyes and let her head fall back against his shoulder. "I just thought Chloe should feel like she had a lot to say in the decision that was going to affect her so profoundly."

He turned her gently to face him. "I think you're right."

Emily caressed the hard muscles of his chest. "I also think she's going to like Sweet Briar Elementary School a lot more than she thinks she's going to."

"I have a feeling she will, too," Edmund agreed gently as he wrapped a comforting arm about her shoulders.

"And if not," Emily continued decisively, "we'll find someplace else for her to go—"

The corners of his mouth crooked up affectionately. "I like the sound of that," he told her playfully as he kneaded his way up and down her spine.

Emily tilted her head, and looked into his eyes, knowing she could drown in their sable brown depths. "The sound of what?" she prodded.

"We." Edmund tugged Emily closer yet. "I like the idea of us doing things together, as a family. I like you taking the place of Chloe's mom in her life."

"I like it, too," Emily whispered, wreathing both her arms around his neck. The knowledge that they had forged such a close, loving bond in so short a time filled her with a happiness and a contentment she'd never expected to have. "I also like Bobby having a daddy in you."

Edmund was euphoric with success, glowing with contentment. "It was pretty neat, wasn't it, when he called me Daddy this morning?"

Emily nodded, knowing it was a moment she'd cherish forever. She was so glad she'd been able to repair that loss in her son's life via Edmund. So glad he now had a father to love and lean on and emulate. "It was indeed," she told him softly.

Edmund lifted her in his arms and carried her the short distance to the bed. Desire swirling in their veins, they kissed and came together in the center of the bed. "Edmund?" Emily murmured when they were naked and yearning again, needing each other with every fiber of their beings.

"Hm?" he said, sliding her over onto her back.

"Do you think things will always be this perfect?" Emily asked as he draped her in warmth, letting her know with every touch, every kiss, every moment he possessed her, just how very much he had come to want and need her in his life.

"No," Edmund teased playfully, molding his body to hers in a heralding of the incredibly slow, incredibly passionate lovemaking to come. "They'll be better."

Chapter Fourteen

"I can't wait to tell Daddy what I decided," Chloe told Emily as they returned home from their school visits late the following afternoon. "Do you think he's going to be happy?"

"Happy about what?" Edmund asked, coming out to the front hall to greet them, Bobby on his hip.

"About the fact I want to enroll in Sweet Briar Elementary—the same place you went to school when you were a kid!" Chloe responded as Maureen came up to join them, too.

"I think that's terrific," Edmund declared.

"So do I," Emily said with a smile.

"What other schools did you see?" Edmund asked, reaching over with his free hand to help Emily off with her coat.

Chloe rattled off the names of the schools, telling Edmund why she had discounted each of the ones not chosen. "Well, it sounds like you made the right choice," Edmund said gravely as Bobby waved at Emily vigorously, then demanded to be put down so he could try walking again.

He took four steps, to the delight of everyone, sat down, then got up and tried again, achieving two more this time. "Hurrah for Bobby!" Maureen declared, every bit the proud and doting grandmother.

Bobby grinned up at Maureen and yelled something completely unintelligible back.

"Don't you wish we could understand everything he's saying?" Maureen said wistfully as she bent and chucked Bobby under the chin.

"It won't be long before we do," Emily predicted, as she and Maureen exchanged woman-to-woman looks, filled with love and joy. The two of them hadn't started out as well as Emily would've liked, but they were fast becoming friends now, and she was very happy about that. It would help her marriage to Edmund a lot to have Maureen in their corner.

Looking pretty happy herself, Chloe tugged on Edmund's sleeve. "Daddy, do you think I could give my snowman a hat and a scarf before he melts?" she asked.

"Sure, pumpkin." Edmund crossed to the front hall closet. "Let me see what's in here."

Finished showing off for the moment, Bobby rubbed his eyes and held out his arms to Emily, signaling he wanted to be picked up. "Did he have a nap?" Emily asked, as she accommodated her son with a smile.

Edmund shook his head and reported with mock seriousness, "He was waiting for you to get home and rock him to sleep."

Emily narrowed her eyes skeptically, and replied in a low, deadpan voice, "Hm. That's a mighty big decision for such a little tyke."

"Okay." Edmund handed Chloe a hat and scarf for her snowman, then turned to Emily with a grin and held up his hands in a time-honored gesture of surrender. "You've got me. I confess. Bobby was having too good a time being the darling of the entire household—" Edmund said.

"And then some," Maureen conceded with a grin.

"—to take his nap," Edmund concluded. "So I didn't even try to put him down."

"Well, he's sleepy now," Emily noted tenderly as Bobby cuddled against her snugly and laid his head on her shoulder. "If you-all don't need me, I think I'll go up and put him down for his nap."

Edmund nodded. "I'll be finishing up a few things in the study."

As Emily expected, it only took about a minute and half of rocking before Bobby was sound asleep. She put him in his crib, covered him with a blanket, then looked around for the baby monitor to switch it on. To her chagrin, it wasn't where it was supposed to be. Figuring Edmund might know where it was, she doubled swiftly back down the stairs and headed for the study.

"Of course, if you'd kept your worries to yourself," Emily overhead Edmund say, "the farm wouldn't have taken such a hit in reputation."

Emily paused. She knew this wasn't a conversation she needed to be part of, but she did need the baby monitor that was very likely in the study with Edmund.

"I'm not sorry it did if it brought you back where you belong," Maureen replied cheerfully. "Thanks to my goof-up, you now have a wife and a son. And if you're very lucky, one day your marriage to Emily will be more than a matter of convenience," she said seriously. "It'll be based on love."

Emily was close enough to the doorway to see Edmund frown unhappily. "My relationship with Emily is just fine as it is, Mother," Edmund said sternly, turning away.

But was it? Emily wondered uneasily, knowing she wanted a lot more than simple friendship, fun, sex and coparenting from their relationship. She'd thought—hoped—Edmund wanted more, too.

"Furthermore," Edmund continued sternly, "I don't want you talking to Emily or me about love or lack thereof."

Which made sense, Emily thought, feeling simultaneously sad and shaken, since he didn't love her. Since he only desired her and needed her to help care for his daughter and recoup the sense of family they'd both lost when their beloved spouses died. They'd done that. Perhaps too well. The honeymoon aspect of the past few days had left her with the misconception that one day Edmund actually might fall in love with her. But as she listened to the blunt, deliberate note in his low voice, she realized that was not going to happen. He was never going to love her. And without love—or even the possibility of it occurring—what kind of marriage could they have? Certainly nothing that would pass the test of time.

Aware she was trembling, she leaned against the wall outside the door and tried to catch her breath.

"My relationship with Emily—with any and all women, for that matter—is off-limits to you. Am I making myself clear?" Edmund asked Maureen.

Perfectly, Emily thought. Figuring she'd heard enough—too much—she turned away.

"SHALL YOU TELL them what we have to celebrate or shall I?" Maureen asked Edmund an hour later as the family gathered in the living room.

Still feeling pretty flush with victory himself, for this latest turn of events would make it easy to hire a top-notch farm manager and hence give him much more time to spend with Emily and the kids, Edmund busied himself filling the glasses. Champagne for the adults, apple juice for the children. "You go ahead," he told his mother happily.

"We won the contract with Mr. and Mrs. King. King's Ransom is going to be put out to stud here."

"Way to go," Gail praised, grinning as she picked up a brimming glass of golden champagne and offered an effusive toast.

"Congratulations," Emily told Edmund, Maureen and Gail as smiles were exchanged all around.

Was it his imagination, Edmund wondered, or was Emily suddenly looking a little tense? One thing was certain—she was going out of her way to avoid looking directly into his eyes.

"The farm is back on top again," Gail presumed happily, as soon as they had toasted the occasion.

Maureen nodded and decreed, "Odds are we'll have all the slots filled for this spring and have the barns at full capacity by the end of next week. Plus we'll have the money for an ad budget, and a few more mares of our own to breed with King's Ransom, and later put up for sale."

"Which also means we won't have to go with Edmund's alternate plan and purchase thirty horses," Gail said.

"Although," Edmund continued with a satisfied smile, glad everything was finally falling into place in a business sense, "we may want to think about gradually doing that anyway, as we can afford it, so we aren't so dependent on outside broodmares to produce foals for our stallions."

"By the way, I ran into the plumber as I was coming up the drive," Gail said. "The work on the cottage is finished. He said you and Emily can move back into it at any time. Even tonight if you want. They dried the carpet, too."

Again, Edmund looked over at Emily. No doubt about it. She did not seem as enthused about the prospect of moving back to the cottage and being alone with him as he had expected she would be, given the intimate turn their relationship had taken the past few days.

Mrs. Hamilton appeared in the doorway. "I've got the evening meal ready for the children, if they'd like to eat a little earlier this evening."

"Good idea," Edmund said quickly. He looked at Gail and his mother. "If you two wouldn't mind overseeing their dinner, I'd like a few minutes alone with Emily." *I'd like to know what's wrong.*

Seconds later, he and Emily were alone in the living room. "Okay, what's the matter?" Edmund asked.

Emily stood, too, and moved as if to evade him. "I have to hunt down the baby monitor."

Edmund sauntered closer. "It's in the study," he said, catching her arm and reeling her back to face him. "And you haven't answered my question."

To his frustration, she stepped back out of reach, folded her arms in front of her and remained silent. Edmund's unhappiness grew as she refused to illuminate him on what had changed her mood so completely. She was acting as if he'd done something wrong! As if he'd hurt her in some way!

"I thought you'd be happy. After all, the Bancrofts are no threat to you now. You have custody of Bobby, and thanks to the trust meant to provide for you and Bobby, you're financially secure."

"You're right," Emily repeated in a brisk, emotional voice. "Everything has worked out. We're free to continue with our lives."

"And our marriage," Edmund added.

At the mention of the vows they had taken, Emily tensed.

And suddenly, Edmund knew. He advanced on her slowly, his eyes holding hers. "That's the problem, isn't it?" Edmund guessed heavily, as dread engulfed him anew. "Our marriage."

Emily swallowed. "I'm grateful for all you've done for me," she began.

Edmund braced his hands on his waist, pushing the edges of his suit coat back. Still eyeing her determinedly, he released a short, impatient breath. "Why does this sound like a kiss-off?"

Maybe because it is. Emily drew a bolstering breath. "I'll be blunt. I'm worried about us, and I'm worried about our children."

"Why?" Edmund closed the distance between them. He cupped her chin with his fingers and turned her face up to his. "Everything's going great. It's only been a couple of days and already Chloe loves you like a mother. Bobby seems to feel the same way about me. He even called me Daddy."

"Exactly." Trembling at his nearness and the intimacy of his touch, Emily turned away from him.

Her heart breaking, she paced away from him. "What's it going to do to them if we ever split up?"

Edmund blinked and regarded her cautiously. "Why would we do that?"

Emily shoved her hands through her hair and struggled with all her might to hold back her tears. "It takes more than just friendship or passion to sustain a marriage, Edmund." She paused, waiting for him to jump in and tell her something that would make her feel less hurt and disillusioned. But as she had feared the moment did not come. "It takes love, Edmund." The one component, apparently, she did not—and could not—engender in him.

Edmund continued staring at her, looking more grim and unhappy than she had ever seen him. "You're telling me you want a divorce?" he asked incredulously.

No, Emily didn't want a divorce! She didn't even want to think about the possibility. But given what she'd overheard him telling his mother, given the fact she'd fallen in love with him, and he didn't love her, didn't even want to discuss the possibility he someday might, what choice did she have but to leave him, now, before it ripped her apart all the more.

Aware she'd never been more miserable, aware she'd never willed anything to work out more, Emily took a deep breath. "I'm telling you the past few days have made me realize that my life isn't over, as I thought. Making love with you has made me realize that I want it all, Edmund, the whole package. Not just friendship and sex, and a two-parent family and a safe place to live. But a husband who loves me, and I can love back." And living without Edmund would be easier than living with him but without his love.

He shot her another baffled look. "If you leave now, the kids will be devastated."

"If I stay, and then leave later, it'll hurt them both all the more." And Emily did not want that. Hands clasped in front of her, she drew another deep breath. "On the other hand, if Bobby and I go tomorrow, it'll hurt them for a while, but then they'll be okay. And so will we. And this way, maybe we can part as friends." *Instead of disillusioned enemies.*

Edmund stared at her, his jaw hardening to the consistency of granite. "This is really what you want?" He pushed the words through a row of even white teeth. "For us to be friends?"

No, Emily thought miserably, it's not what I want at all, but it's what has to be. She lifted her shoulders in an insouciant shrug, knowing even as she spoke, it sounded like a kiss-off, an inordinately cruel kiss-off. "I still think we have a lot in common."

He looked away, the depth of his weariness apparent. He turned back to her, a stoic look in his sable brown eyes. "All right then." He looked at her as if she had just sealed the lid on her own coffin. "If that's what you want, I won't stand in your way," he promised brusquely.

"Thank you." She should have known she could count on him to be a gentleman to the last, even if it wasn't what he wanted, now anyway.

A heartrending silence fell between them. "About tonight—" she said after a moment.

For one brief second, he looked as if he wanted to shake her, kiss her—anything to change her mind. "What about it?" he demanded gruffly.

Emily swallowed. As difficult as it was for both of them, she knew she was doing the right thing.

"As long as the caretaker's cottage is available, I was wondering if Bobby and I might stay there."

"I CAN'T BELIEVE YOU and Edmund are splitting up now, after all you've been through," Gail said, as she helped Emily carry the last of her things into the cottage and put a sleeping Bobby in his crib there.

Emily paused to cover Bobby with a blanket, then eased out of the room. "We never should have gotten married."

"I agree it looked foolish at the time," Gail argued.

"It was foolish then and it's foolish now." Emily walked into the kitchen to put some water on for tea.

"He loves you," Gail said.

Dream on. Aware they were headed into dangerous territory—territory that could easily make her cry— Emily concentrated on measuring tea into the pot. "Then why hasn't he ever said the words?" Emily gave Edmund's sister a quelling look.

Gail flushed. She crossed over to the window and stood looking out at the thick blanket of snow still covering the ground and obscuring the trees. "Well, I can't answer that."

Emily angled a thumb at her chest. "And we still barely know each other."

Gail shook her head at Emily disparagingly. "I still think you're making a mistake. You haven't given the marriage a chance."

Emily sighed. "I know how real the marriage looked. For a few days there, it even fooled me. But in reality it was nothing but a cure for our mutual loneliness. A way to bring us out of our memories with our spouses, and back to the present again."

"I don't believe that, and neither should you."

Emily took a deep breath and through sheer force of will, pushed back the tears gathering in her eyes. Still struggling to compose herself, she turned away from the mixture of sadness and pity in Gail's eyes. "I don't want to believe it," Emily said hoarsely.

"But you do," Gail guessed.

"Yes," Emily admitted miserably. Like it or not, there were some things you couldn't wish into reality, through sheer strength of will and gritty determination; this just happened to be one of them.

"Listen to me, Emily." Gail curved a compassionate hand over her forearm and forced her to face her. "You're a fool if you let a love like this slip through your fingers. Whether Edmund has said the words to you or not, he does love you. I know it in here." Gail laid a hand over her heart. "Otherwise he never would have gone all out to make you his, even if he was Brian's friend, and you were a damsel in distress!"

"GAIL IS BACK FROM the cottage," Maureen announced from the doorway of the study.

Edmund sat back in his chair. "Did Emily get settled okay?" he asked gruffly.

His mother nodded as she carried in the tray of coffee and cookies and set it down on the edge of his desk. "Apparently."

"Good." Edmund went back to his work. "Thanks for the coffee."

As he had feared, his mother did not take the hint and she did not leave. "Are you sure you know what you're doing?" she asked as she poured him a cup of coffee from the silver tea service and set it at his elbow.

Figuring she wouldn't leave until she'd had her say, Edmund leaned back in his chair. "What do you mean?"

"Throwing her out this way."

"I told you, Mother." Edmund sighed and lifted the delicate china cup to his lips. "I did not ask Emily to leave. She told me she was going."

His mother poured herself some coffee, stirred in sugar, and eased down into a chair opposite him. "Same thing," she said.

Edmund frowned. "Not in my book."

"Did you do anything to stop her?" Maureen persisted.

Edmund rolled his eyes. "You mean throw myself down in front of the Jeep and beg her not to go?"

"Yes." Maureen waited hopefully.

"No," Edmund told her tersely. "I didn't."

Maureen frowned. "And why not?" she demanded, disappointed.

Edmund scowled. "That's not the kind of arrangement we had."

"I see."

Edmund tensed. "What's that tone of voice supposed to mean?" he demanded.

His mother was all innocence. "Nothing," she said sweetly.

"Just spit it out." Edmund quaffed his coffee so quickly he burned his mouth. "I know you're dying to tell me."

Settling her cup and saucer on her knee, Maureen leaned forward urgently. "Look, darling, I know you're an excellent businessman and a wonderful father, but you are missing a very important part of the big picture here."

Like hell he was, Edmund thought. He knew when he'd been given the boot. "And that is…?"

"You and Emily have invested a lot into this relationship."

Heaven knew he'd given it his heart and soul. "Your point being?" Edmund demanded gruffly.

"Maybe you should keep trying."

Edmund stood abruptly and began to pace. "She doesn't love me, Mother."

Maureen made a pooh-poohing gesture. "Who told you that?"

Edmund blew out a gusty breath, still unable to believe how much it had hurt, hearing she didn't want to be married to him any longer. "She did."

"She came out and said that?" Maureen fixed him with a disbelieving look.

Edmund frowned, and paced to the window. Snow glistened on the ground—not unlike the ice already forming around his heart. "Not exactly." Edmund stared out at the moonlight. He wished he could turn back the clock, to the start of the blizzard. He wished he knew what he'd done wrong, so he could rewrite history, but that was ridiculous. He knew—more painfully than most—there were no do-overs in this life.

"What did she say then—exactly?" Maureen pressed.

Edmund released an exasperated breath and pivoted back around to face Maureen. "That we no longer needed each other—it was time we moved on—we both deserved more out of life. Stuff like that."

The worst part of it was, Edmund thought on a new wave of frustration, he hadn't seen it coming. Not for one second. Damn it all, what was it with him? How could he be so clueless? He'd thought Emily was content with the way things were in their marriage. But she hadn't been. And as usual, he was the last to know. The only way he'd figured out she was holding back on him was when someone else—in this case Emily herself—spelled it out for him. And even then he hadn't wanted to see it or believe it.

"What else did she say?" Maureen asked.

Edmund began to pace again. "Determined to torture me, aren't you, Mother?"

"Yes. Go on."

In a voice dripping with sarcasm, Edmund recounted, "She said she was grateful for all I'd done for her." Damn it all to hell, he wondered how long Emily'd been rehearsing that speech.

"And?" Maureen prodded impatiently.

"And it takes more than passion to sustain a marriage."

Maureen continued to purse her lips and look thoughtful. "Anything else?"

Edmund shrugged. What else was there? "She wants the whole package. Not just friendship and sex and a two-parent family and a safe place to live. But a mate she can love totally."

Maureen began to smile. For the life of him, he couldn't figure out why. "Maybe she's changed her mind by now," Maureen suggested optimistically. "Maybe she doesn't really want to leave."

And Edmund'd thought he was dense. "Didn't you hear anything I said?"

"I heard everything, dear." Maureen rose with regal grace. She patted him reassuringly on the hand. "I also heard what you didn't say."

"That being?" Edmund watched her gather the cups and saucers and put them back on the tray.

"That you love Emily. But you do, don't you?"

Edmund scowled. "Well, yes—"

Maureen's brows drew together disapprovingly. "And ten to one, you've never told her, have you?"

Edmund flushed as his gaze fell on the baby monitor still on his desk. If he wasn't so desperate to have Emily back, there was no way he'd be discussing this! "We only knew each other a few days!"

"And yet you married her and, judging from the looks of things, even made love to her."

The pain he'd felt at her rejection came back full force. Edmund ground the words between his teeth. "It was a mistake," he said grimly.

Maureen shook her head. "Loving someone is never a mistake, dear. Loving them—and not telling them so—is."

LOVING SOMEONE is never a mistake, dear. Loving them—and not telling them so—is.

His mother was right, Edmund thought, as he pocketed the baby monitor Emily had accidentally left behind and went for his coat and car keys. If he didn't do something drastic and do it soon, he really would lose Emily forever.

So maybe there were things wrong with their relationship thus far. Maybe he hadn't naturally intuited everything he needed to know about her and her feelings. It didn't mean he couldn't learn, did it? It didn't mean theirs was a hopeless case. He headed for the door before he lost his nerve, hoping it still wasn't too late.

Emily answered on the first knock at the cottage

door. She was still wearing the pale pink cashmere cardigan and matching sweater set, and coordinating white wool slacks, she'd had on earlier in the day.

Her black hair fell in loose tousled waves about her face and shoulders. She looked incredibly lovely but, to Edmund's chagrin, there was nothing of what she was thinking or feeling on her face. He was going to have to do this on instinct alone. Not necessarily a good sign.

Edmund held up the baby monitor. "I found this on the desk in the study and thought you might need it."

"Oh, thanks." Shivering in the cold biting wind, she ushered him in, shut the door behind him, but— to Edmund's growing disappointment—made no move to immediately take his coat.

So what? Edmund thought. He'd known, coming over here, this wasn't going to be easy. Not by a long shot.

"Is Bobby still asleep?" Edmund asked, edging nearer.

Emily nodded. "He's exhausted. I don't imagine he'll wake up all night," Emily confided in a soft, husky tone as she turned to face him. Her tongue darted out to moisten her softly glossed lips. "What about Chloe?"

"Out like a light." Figuring if ever there was a time to be presumptuous, this was it, Edmund took off his coat and draped it over a chair. "My mother and Gail are keeping an ear out for her."

She swallowed, studying him, gauging the reason for his presence. "What's going on?"

"I hoped we might talk."

Emily ran a hand through her hair, abruptly looking

as nervous and on edge as he felt. "Actually," she said softly, still holding his eyes. "I was hoping we could talk, too."

Edmund held up a hand before she could proceed. "But first I have some things I want to say," he interjected as he took her hand and led her to the sofa in front of the fire. "I know now I should never have asked you to marry me the way I did. But I can't go back and change that now, any more than I can change the blizzard that's inundated us for days."

Emily interrupted, taking both his hands in both of hers. "Neither of us can." She took a deep breath and looked into his eyes, before finishing determinedly, "We're just going to have to go on."

"That's just it," Edmund said. "I don't want to go from here to divorce. And I sure as heck don't want to go back to being just friends."

Emily held herself very still. Some of the light left her sea blue eyes. "You don't."

"No," Edmund said gruffly, "I don't. I have to be honest with you, Emily." He knew he had to just throw it all out there, and let the chips fall where they may. "After what we shared, I don't think we could ever go back to a platonic relationship. We're sort of at an all-or-nothing stage."

"I see," Emily said coldly. Extracting her hands from his, she stood and began to pace.

Did she? He didn't think so.

Edmund stood, crossed to her side, and tried again. "Look—" he put up both hands in a gesture of surrender "—I know we just had a couple of days together. But we were a good team—"

"Right," Emily interrupted again. "But I can't go on being your wife."

Here it was. The golden opportunity. The time to lay it all on the line and hope like hell she at least liked him enough to give him a second chance.

"Not even if I love you with all my heart and soul?" Edmund asked softly.

Emily blinked and could not have looked more stunned. "What did you say?" she whispered disbelievingly.

"That I love you," Edmund repeated hoarsely, containing his urge to shout it to the world only because of the baby sleeping in the next room. He cupped her arms with his hands. "Did you hear me, Emily? I love you and I always will. I know you don't feel the same—"

She held up a hand. "Edmund. Wait—"

He silenced her with a fingertip pressed to her lips. "No. You wait. I have to tell you this, Emily." I have to say it all before I lose my nerve. "I don't know how it happened or why, but I felt a connection with you, the first time we wrote letters to each other after Brian's and Lindsey's deaths. And that connection deepened when we talked about how we were each handling our grief and spoke on the phone, and it deepened even more when you wanted the job as Chloe's nanny. By the time you showed up on my doorstep, the wheels for our involvement were already set in motion. I knew there was something there—something special—so special I couldn't let you leave." Edmund paused. "I have to be honest. I would've done anything to get you—and Bobby—to stay with us. Marrying you was nothing. But even that didn't go the way I figured it would because the moment I held you in my arms and kissed you, I knew this was no ordinary platonic thing. This was real.

This involved hearts and minds and souls. And that was a shock, too. When I lost Lindsey, I swore I'd never love again. I meant it. I was sure of it. I know you felt the same way about Brian, when you lost him.''

"I did." Emily's eyes were overflowing, her voice was clogged with tears.

"But Brian would want you to go on with your life, just as I know Lindsey would want me to go on with mine.''

Emily nodded, as her sadness gave way to serenity. "I know that, too," she whispered resolutely.

"More to the point, I think they'd want us to be together.''

Emily wiped her eyes, looking for a moment both amused and exasperated. "Doesn't it matter how I feel about all this?" she cried.

"Of course.''

Emily folded her arms in front of her and continued to regard him warily. "And finally you're going to allow me to get a word in edgewise?''

Edmund took a deep, reluctant breath. "Go ahead.''

"I didn't tell you I wanted our marriage to end because I wanted it to be over," Emily explained, in the soft serious voice he had come to love. "I did it because I felt I had to, because I didn't want a marriage without love.''

"But I do love you!''

Tears flowed freely. She went toward him, arms outstretched. He wrapped her in his arms. She clung tightly. "I know that, now." Her voice was muffled against his chest. "And I love you.''

Edmund blinked. Not sure he hadn't imagined it.

"What?" he asked hoarsely, and was rewarded by the sound of her soft, melodic laughter.

"We both seem to be having a little trouble comprehending those words tonight, don't we?" she teased, as she drew back, and wreathed her arms around his neck. "So maybe..." Emily said as she stood on tiptoe, ran her fingers through his dark windswept hair, and looked deep into his eyes "...I should just show you instead."

"Show me how?" Edmund said, sweeping a hand down her spine, already beginning to like this very much.

"Like this." Emily delivered a soul-searing kiss. "And this." She delivered another and another. Taking him by the hand, she led him into the bedroom he had once occupied alone. "And this," she said, as she began to undo his tie.

"Emily..."

"We want all the same things, Edmund. Home, family—"

"Maybe even another child," Edmund supposed as the two of them leisurely undressed and swept back the covers.

Emily grinned as they landed on the bed. "Definitely another child."

"So when the time is right—" Edmund took her into his arms once again.

"We'll work on it," Emily promised.

"Definitely work on it," Edmund agreed as they came together, opening themselves up to each other, loving each other heart, body and soul.

"Emily?" Edmund said drowsily, a long time later, as unwilling to untangle their bodies as she.

Replete from their lovemaking, Emily cuddled

close and rested her head on his chest. It was hard to imagine in the space of one fierce winter storm, all her dreams could come true, but they had. "Hm?"

"Before we get started again," Edmund teased adoringly. He cupped a hand under her chin, tipped her face up to his, and looked down at her with serious sable brown eyes. "I love you. I love you. I love you. I love you."

Tears of happiness spilled down Emily's face. They had their whole lifetimes ahead of them, not to mention all the fun, friendship, passion, love and joy marriage had to offer. "Edmund?"

"Hm?"

She shifted her body overtop of his, wreathed her arms around his neck and kissed him back with all the love and tenderness she possessed. This was just the beginning and it was only going to get better. "I love you, too."

FIVE STARS
MEAN SUCCESS

If you see the "5 Star Club" flash on a book,
it means we're introducing you to one of our
most STELLAR authors!

Every one of our Harlequin and Silhouette
authors who has sold over 5 MILLION BOOKS
has been selected for our "5 Star Club."

We've created the club so you won't miss
any of our bestsellers. So, each month
we'll be highlighting every original book within
Harlequin and Silhouette written by our
bestselling authors.

NOW THERE'S NO WAY ON EARTH OUR
STARS WON'T BE SEEN!

OVER
5 MILLION
BOOKS SOLD
SPECIAL OFFER INSIDE

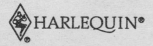

HARLEQUIN®   Silhouette®

P5STAR

This April
DEBBIE MACOMBER

takes readers to the Big Sky and beyond...

MONTANA

At her grandfather's request, Molly packs up her kids and returns to his ranch in Sweetgrass, Montana.

But when she arrives, she finds a stranger, Sam Dakota, working there. Molly has questions: What exactly is he doing there? Why doesn't the sheriff trust him? Just *who* is Sam Dakota? These questions become all the more critical when her grandfather tries to push them into marriage....

Moving to the state of Montana is one thing; entering the state of matrimony is quite another!

Available in April 1998 wherever books are sold.

Catch more great

HARLEQUIN™ Movies

featured on themovie channel tmc

Premiering April 11th
Hard to Forget
based on the novel by bestselling
Harlequin Superromance® author
Evelyn A. Crowe

Don't miss next month's movie!
Premiering May 9th
The Awakening
starring Cynthia Geary and David Beecroft
based on the novel by Patricia Coughlin

If you are not currently a subscriber to
The Movie Channel, simply call your
local cable or satellite provider for more
details. Call today, and don't miss out
on the romance!

themovie channel tmc
100% pure movies.
100% pure fun.

HARLEQUIN™
Makes any time special™

An Alliance Television Production

HMBPA498